THE BRAID

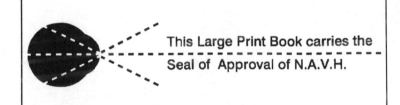

This Large Print Book carries the
Seal of Approval of N.A.V.H.

THE BRAID

LAETITIA COLOMBANI

THORNDIKE PRESS
A part of Gale, a Cengage Company

GALE
A Cengage Company

LIBRARY OF CONGRESS CIP DATA ON FILE.
CATALOGUING IN PUBLICATION FOR THIS BOOK
IS AVAILABLE FROM THE LIBRARY OF CONGRESS

ISBN-13: 978-1-4328-7236-6 (hardcover alk. paper)

Published in 2020 by arrangement with Atria Books, an imprint of Simon & Schuster, Inc.

Printed in Mexico
1 2 3 4 5 6 7 24 23 22 21 20

For Olivia,
and all women of courage

Braid, v.
To form (three or more strands) into a
braid; to do up (the hair) by interweaving
three or more strands

There is great mystery, Simone, in the
forest of your hair.

REMY DE GOURMONT

A free woman is precisely the opposite of
a light woman.

SIMONE DE BEAUVOIR

PROLOGUE

The beginning of a story. A new story,
  each time.
Coming to life, at my fingertips.

First, the frame.
A structure strong enough to support the
  whole.
Silk or cotton for the city, or the setting,
  as required.
Cotton is strong,
Silk is finer, more discreet.
I need a hammer and nails.
I need, above all, to proceed slowly,
  gently.

Next, the weaving.
The part I like best.
Before me, on the loom,
Three nylon threads are stretched.
Taking the strands from the skein,
Three by three;

Knotting them carefully, so they don't
    break.
And then repeat.
Thousands of times over.

I love these solitary hours, these hours
    when my hands dance.
The strange ballet of my fingers.
They tell a story of intertwining strands.
This story is mine.

But does not belong to me.

SMITA

A village in Badlapur, Uttar Pradesh, India
Smita wakes with a strange feeling. Urgent, gentle, new: butterflies in her stomach. Today is a day she will remember her whole life. Today, her daughter will go to school.

School, where Smita has never set foot. Here in Badlapur, people like her don't go to school. Smita is a Dalit. Of those whom Mahatma Gandhi called Harijan, the Children of God. "The oppressed." Untouchable. Unworthy. A species apart, judged too impure to mix with others, rejected and separated, like the chaff from the wheat. Millions like Smita live outside the villages, outside society: on the margins of humanity.

Every morning, the ritual is the same. Like a scratched record playing the same hellish music over and over again. Smita wakes in the hut that is her home, beside the fields cultivated by the Jatts. She washes her face

13

and hands in the water fetched the day before from the well set aside for her people. No question of using the other well, the one for the higher castes, though it is nearer and easier to reach. People have died for less. Smita makes herself ready, does Lalita's hair, kisses Nagarajan. Then she takes the rush basket that her mother carried before her. The very sight of it makes her retch. *The hateful basket with its persistent, indelible smell, the thing she carries with her all day, her shameful burden. A punishment. A curse. For something she did in a* past life. She must pay, atone for the sin. Because this life is no more important than the others that came before it, or the lives to come. It's just one life among many, her mother would say. This is how life is — her life.

This is her dharma, her duty, her place in the world. A task handed down from mother to daughter, for generations. Manual scavenger: a coy term that bears little relation to reality. There are other words to describe what Smita does for a living: she collects other people's shit, removing it barehanded from the dry latrines, using only a stiff reed brush and a metal scoop, all day long. She was six years old — the same age Lalita is now — when her mother took her along for

14

the first time. Watch, then you will do the same. Smita remembers the smell that assaulted her, sharp and violent as a swarm of wasps, an unbearable, bestial stench. She had vomited on the side of the road. You'll get used to it, her mother said. She had lied. You never get used to it. Smita learned to hold her breath, to live without breathing. You must breathe freely, the village doctor told her, see how you're coughing. You must eat. Smita lost her appetite long ago. She no longer remembers what it is to feel hungry. She eats little, the strict minimum, forcing it down in spite of herself every day.

And yet the government promised toilets, right across the country. They have not come here. In Badlapur, as elsewhere, people defecate in the open. The ground is filthy, everywhere: the streams and rivers, the fields, polluted with tons of excrement. Sickness spreads like wildfire. The politicians know it: what people want, before reforms or social equality, are toilets. The right to defecate with dignity. In the villages, many women are forced to wait until nightfall, to go out into the fields, exposing themselves to the risk of attack. The most fortunate have a corner set aside in their yard, or at the back of their house: a simple hole in the ground, euphemistically described as a "dry latrine." These are the latrines that the Dalit women come to empty every day, barehanded. Women like Smita.

She begins her rounds at about seven o'clock in the morning. Smita takes her basket lined with ashes, her scoop, and her stiff reed brush. She has twenty houses to empty, every day, no time to lose. She walks along the side of the road, eyes lowered, her face hidden in her scarf. In some villages, Dalits are forced to wear crows' feathers as a mark of their status. Elsewhere, they must walk barefoot. Everyone knows the story of the Dalit who was stoned merely for wearing sandals. Smita enters the houses by the door reserved for her kind, at the back. She mustn't cross the path of the people living there, let alone speak to them. She is not only untouchable: she must be invisible, too. By way of a salary, she receives leftover food, sometimes old clothes tossed onto the floor for her to pick up. No touching, no looking. And sometimes a few rupees. Sometimes she gets nothing at all. One family of Jatts has given her nothing for months. Smita wanted to stop; she said so one night to Nagarajan. She wouldn't go back there — they could clean their own shit. But Nagarajan had been afraid. If Smita stopped

16

going there, they would be chased out: they have no piece of land to call their own. The Jatts would come and burn their hut. Smita knew what they were capable of. "We'll cut off both your legs," they had said to one of her kind. The man had been found in a nearby field, dismembered and burned with acid.

Yes, Smita knew what the Jatts were capable of. And so she went back to the house the next day.

But this morning is not like every other day. Smita has made a decision. The obvious choice, the only one possible: her daughter will go to school. She had trouble persuading Nagarajan. What would be the point? he said. She might learn how to read and write, but no one will give her work. You are born to empty latrines, and you do it until you die. It's your heritage, a circle no one can break. *Karma.*

Smita didn't give in. She brought it up again the next day, the day after, and every day after that. She refused to take Lalita with her on her rounds: she would not show her how to clear toilets, she would not watch while her daughter vomited into the ditch, as her mother had watched before her. No, Smita could not do that. Lalita must go to school. In the face of her determination,

Nagarajan had relented. He knew his wife; Smita had a will of iron. The small, dark-skinned Dalit woman he had married ten years ago was stronger than him, he knew that. And so he gave in. This is how it would be: he would go to the village school. He would speak to the Brahmin.

Smita smiled secretly at her victory. She so wished her mother had felt able to fight for her; she so longed to have walked through the school gates and taken her place with the other children. To have learned to read and write. But it wasn't possible. Smita's father wasn't like Nagarajan; he had been irascible, and violent. He beat his wife, like so many men here. He repeated it often enough: a woman is not her husband's equal. She is his property, his slave. She must do his bidding. Her father would sooner have saved his cow than his wife.

But Smita has been fortunate: Nagarajan has never beaten her, never insulted her. When Lalita was born, he even agreed to keep her. Not far away, girls are killed at birth. In villages in Rajasthan, newborn girls are buried alive in a box under the sand. The babies take a whole night to die.

But not here. Smita gazes at Lalita, squatting on the beaten earth floor of their hut, combing her only doll's hair. Truly, her

18

daughter is beautiful. She has delicate features and hair down to her waist. Smita brushes it out and braids it every morning.

My daughter will learn how to read and write, she tells herself, and she rejoices at the thought.

Yes, today is a day she will remember all her life.

GIULIA

Palermo, Sicily

"Giulia!"

Giulia struggled to open her eyes. Her mother's voice called up the stairs.

"Giulia! *Scendi! Subito!*"

Giulia was tempted to bury her head under the pillow. She'd had too little sleep — another night spent reading. But she knew she must get up. When Mamma calls, you obey — especially if she is Sicilian.

"Giulia!"

Reluctantly, she got out of bed, dressed quickly, and went down to the kitchen, where her mother waited impatiently. Her sister Adela was already down and painting her toenails, with one foot up on the table. Giulia winced at the smell of the polish. Her mother poured her a cup of coffee.

"Your father's gone out already. You'll be opening up this morning."

Giulia took the keys to the workshop and

hurried out of the house.

"You've had nothing to eat! Take something with you!"

Ignoring her mother's words, Giulia jumped onto her bike and pedaled away, hard. She felt more awake now, in the cool morning air. The sea breeze blew along the streets, stinging her face and eyes. Approaching the market, she smelled the tang of citrus fruit and olives. Giulia pedaled past the fishmonger's stall with its display of freshly caught sardines and eels. She rode faster, mounted the pavements, left Piazza Ballaro behind, where the street vendors were already calling out to their clientele.

She turned onto a dead-end lane off the Via Roma. Her father's workshop was here, in an old cinema building he had bought two decades ago, the year Giulia was born. Back then, he had been operating out of smaller premises and needed to move somewhere bigger. The facade still bore the frames where film posters used to be displayed. The days were long gone when the *Palermitani* would jostle for tickets to see comedies starring Alberto Sordi, Vittorio Gassman, Nino Manfredi, Ugo Tognazzi, or Marcello Mastroianni. Most of the cinemas had closed down, just like this little neighborhood movie theater had done. The old projection room had been turned into an office, and windows had been cut into the auditorium walls to give the women enough light to work by. Papà had put them in himself. The place was like him, Giulia thought: rough-edged and warm. Pietro Lanfredi was liked and respected by his employees, despite his legendary rages. He was a loving father, but authoritarian, too, with high standards. He had brought up his daughters to respect discipline, given them his taste for hard work and a job well done.

Giulia took the key and opened the door. Usually, her father was the first to arrive. He liked to greet his workers in person — that's what a proper padrone does, he would say. Always a kind word for one of the women, a thoughtful gesture for another, a moment's attention for everyone. But today was his day for making the rounds of the hair salons of Palermo and the surrounding villages. He wouldn't be back before noon. This morning, Giulia was in charge.

All was quiet in the workshop at this hour. Soon the place would be humming with voices, singing, scraps of conversation, but for now there were only Giulia's footsteps, echoing in the silence. She walked to the workers' changing room and stowed her things in the locker bearing her name. She took her smock and slipped it on, as she did every day, like a second skin. She gathered her hair, rolled it into a tight chignon, and pinned it with nimble fingers. Then she covered her head with a scarf — an essential precaution here. No stray strands could be allowed to mingle with the hair being treated at the workshop. Dressed and scarved, she was no longer the padrone's daughter; she was a worker like any other, an employee of the House of Lanfredi. This was important to her — she had always refused special treatment of any kind.

The main door creaked open, and a bright swarm swept into the empty space. In an instant, the workshop sprang to life and became the bustling place Giulia loved so much. In a hubbub of conversation, the women hurried to the changing room, donned their smocks and aprons, and reported to their stations, talking all the while. Giulia joined them. Agnese's features were tired and drawn — her youngest was teething, she hadn't slept all night. Federica was holding back her tears — her fiancé had left. Alda was indignant — again?! He'll be back tomorrow, Paola reassured her. The women shared more than their work here. While their busy hands treated the hair, they talked about men and life and love, all day long. Here, everyone knew that Gina's husband drank; that Alda's son was caught in the tentacles of the mafia; that Alessia had had a short-lived affair with Rhina's ex-husband; and that Rhina had never forgiven her.

Giulia loved the company of these women. Some had known her since she was a child. She had almost been born here, at the workshop. Her mother liked to tell everyone how the contractions had caught her by surprise when she was busy sorting the skeins of hair in the main atelier. She had given up work now; her poor eyesight had forced her to step aside to make way for a new, sharper-eyed employee. Giulia had grown up surrounded by the hair waiting to be combed out, the strands ready to be washed, the orders prepared for dispatch. She remembered holidays and days off school spent among the women, watching them work. She loved to see their hands darting busily back and forth, like an army of ants. She watched them draw the hair through the cards — the big, square combs that remove the tangles — before washing it in the great vat on its trestle support, an ingenious solution assembled by her father, who didn't like to see his employees straining their backs. Giulia smiled to see the bunches of hair hanging up in the windows to dry, like a series of bizarre trophies — the scalps in an old Western movie.

Sometimes, it seemed to Giulia that time stood still here. Outside, everything went on as normal, but inside these walls she felt protected. It was a gentle, comforting feeling. The certainty of a strange kind of permanence.

For more than a century now, her family had made its living from the *cascatura,* the old Sicilian custom of keeping hair after it has fallen out or been cut, in order to make hairpieces or wigs. The Lanfredi workshop was the last of its kind in Palermo. Ten expert workers disentangled, washed, and treated the skeins, which were dispatched to wig makers across Italy and the whole of Europe. On her sixteenth birthday, Giulia had decided to leave school and join her father in the workshop. Her teachers said she was a gifted student, especially her Italian teacher, who urged her to continue her education — she could have gone to university. But nothing would dissuade Giulia from her chosen path. Hair was more than a tradition for the Lanfredi; it was a passion, passed down from generation to generation. Oddly, Giulia's sisters showed no interest whatsoever in the family business.

She was the only Lanfredi daughter to take it up. Francesca had married young and didn't go out to work: she had four children now. Adela, the youngest, was still at school and had set her sights on a career in fashion, or modeling. Anything other than joining the workshop.

For special orders and unusual colors, Papà had a secret: a formula inherited from his father, and his grandfather before him, based on natural ingredients whose names were a closely guarded secret. This was the formula he had passed on to Giulia. Often, he would take her up to his attic *laboratorio,* as he called it. You could see the sea from there, and Monte Pellegrino on the other side. Dressed in a white coat that made him look like a Chemistry teacher, Pietro would boil up his mixture in huge pans. He knew how to bleach hair and dye it again so that the new color would hold fast when washed. Giulia studied the process for hours, attentive to his slightest movement. Her father watched the pans of hair like her mother watched the pasta on the stove. He stirred the hair with a wooden paddle, left it to stand, then stirred it again, tirelessly, over and over. He was patient and painstaking, and there was love and care in his handling of the hair. One day, he liked to say, this hair will be worn. It deserves the greatest respect. Sometimes, Giulia found herself daydreaming about the women who would wear the finished wigs. Sicilian men didn't tend to wear hairpieces — they were too proud, too attached to their idea of virility.

For unknown reasons, some hair resisted the Lanfredis' secret formula. Most strands would be immersed in the pans and emerge milky white, ready to be dyed anew, but a few would retain their original color. These rebel hairs posed a very real problem: it was unthinkable for a client to find a rogue black or brown hair in a meticulously dyed skein of blond. The delicate task fell to Giulia, with her very sharp eyes: she would sort the hairs, one by one, and weed out the stubborn individualists. It was a merciless, meticulous witch hunt, pursued day after day.

Paola's voice interrupted her reverie.

"*Mia cara,* you look tired. You've been up all night reading again."

Giulia didn't bother to deny it. There was nothing you could hide from Paola. The old lady was the doyenne of the workforce. Everyone called her La Nonna. She had known Giulia's father when he was a boy, and liked to tell everyone how she used to tie his shoelaces for him. From the vantage

27

point of her seventy-five years, there was nothing she did not see. Her hands were worn, her skin was wrinkled like parchment, but her eyes were still piercingly sharp. Widowed at twenty-five, she had raised four children alone, refusing ever to remarry. When asked why, she would say she cherished her freedom: a married woman was accountable, she said. Do whatever you like, *mia cara,* she would tell Giulia, but above all, never marry. She often talked about her marriage, to a man chosen by her father. Her future husband's family were lemon growers. La Nonna was made to work gathering the fruit, even on her wedding day. There was no rest in the countryside. She remembered the smell of lemons, forever on her husband's hands and clothes. When he died of pneumonia only a few years later, leaving her alone with four children, she was forced to move to the town and look for work. That was when she met Giulia's grandfather, who hired her for his workshop. Five decades had passed, and she was still employed there.

"You won't find a husband in a book!" Alda told Giulia, laughing.

"Leave her in peace," grumbled La Nonna.

Giulia wasn't looking for a husband. She

never went to the cafés or nightclubs where people her age spent their time. Mamma made excuses for her "unsociable" daughter. Giulia preferred the quiet of the *biblioteca communale* to the racket of the discotheque and spent her lunch break there every day. She was a voracious reader, and loved the stillness of the big, book-lined rooms, disturbed only by the rustle of turning pages. There was something religious about the place, it seemed to her — a mystical, meditative atmosphere that she loved. When she was reading, Giulia never noticed time passing. As a child, sitting in the workshop at the women's feet, she had devoured the swashbuckling adventures of Emilio Salgari. Later, she discovered poetry. She liked Caproni better than Ungaretti, and Moravia's prose, and above all Pavese, permanently on her bedside table. She felt she could spend her whole life in his company. Sitting in the library, she would often forget to eat, and she would come back from her lunch break with an empty stomach. That's how it was: Giulia devoured books like other people devoured cannoli.

When she returned that afternoon, it was to a strange silence in the main workshop. All eyes turned to her as she entered.

"Mia cara," said La Nonna, in an unfamil-

iar voice. "Your mamma has just called. It's your father . . . ."

SARAH

Montreal, Canada

The alarm sounded and the countdown began. Sarah's life was relentless, from the moment she woke to the moment she went to bed. The instant she opened her eyes, her brain started to whir like the processor in her computer.

She got up at five every morning. No time for more sleep, every second counted. Her day was a race against the second hand, calibrated down to the last inch, like the pads of graph paper she bought each year at the end of summer vacation for the children's math classes. Her carefree, spontaneous days were long gone: the days before the firm, before motherhood and responsibility. The days when a telephone call could change everything. Tonight, how about . . . ? What if we . . . ? Do you feel like going to . . . ? Now, everything was planned, organized, anticipated. No room for making it up as you went along. You learned your role, and you played it over and over, day after day, week in, month out, all year round. Mother, professional, boss, Wonder Woman, all the labels the magazines loved to pin on women like her, as burdensome as the tote bags they slung over their shoulders.

Sarah got out of bed, showered, and dressed. Her movements were precise, efficient, preprogrammed, like a musician in a military marching band. Down in the kitchen, she laid the breakfast table, always in the same order: milk/bowls/orange juice/chocolate powder. Pancakes for Hannah and Simon, cereal for Ethan, a double espresso for her.

Then she would go wake up the children: Hannah first, then the twins. Their clothes for the day were laid out the night before by Ron. All they had to do was wash their faces and dress while Hannah did the lunch boxes. Fast and smooth, like Sarah's sedan gliding through their neighborhood streets on the school run. Simon and Ethan in elementary school; Hannah in high school, now.

Pecks on the cheek. Have you got everything? You'll be cold, put on that sweater. Good luck on your math test! That's enough back there. No, you're going to gym class today. And last but not least, the traditional reminder: you're all at your dads' places next weekend. Then the drive to the office.

At eight thirty sharp, she would drive into the parking lot and pull up in front of the sign that bore her name.

"Sarah Cohen, Johnson and Lockwood." She looked at it every morning with a touch of pride, the plaque that indicated so much more than her own personal parking space. She was a partner, she had a place in the world. Her accomplishment. Her life's work. Success. Her realm.

The doorman greeted her in the foyer, followed by the girl at the front desk. Always the same ritual. She was universally liked. Sarah entered the elevator, pressed the button for the eighth floor, walked quickly down the hallways to her office. There were never many others around. She was often the first in and the last to leave. That was the price you paid to build a career, to become Sarah Cohen, equity partner in Johnson & Lockwood, one of the city's most respected and prestigious firms. Women were in the majority further down the ranks, but Sarah was the only one to have made partner in a firm that had a reputation for machismo.

Most of her girlfriends from law school had hit the glass ceiling. Some had even given up, changed careers, despite their long, hard years of study. Not her. Not Sarah Cohen. She had shattered the glass ceiling, blow by blow, with her overtime, her weekends at the office, the sleepless nights preparing her pleas. She remembered the first time she had walked into the huge marble foyer, ten years ago. Called in for an interview, she had faced a panel of eight men, including Johnson, the eponymous founder and managing partner. God himself, come down from his office to the conference room especially for the occasion. He hadn't spoken a word, but had fixed her with his hard stare, poring over her résumé line by line, making no comment. Sarah had felt unsettled but refused to show it.

She was skilled at composing a mask, practiced in the art for years now. When the interview was over, she had felt vaguely discouraged. Johnson had asked no questions, demonstrated not a glimmer of interest. Like a hardened poker player, he had shown no expression during the interview, and uttered nothing but a terse "Goodbye," leaving her with little hope of success. Sarah knew there were plenty of other candidates for the job. She had applied from another, smaller, less prestigious firm. Nothing was certain. Others would have more experience, more fighting spirit, a better chance.

Later, she found out that Johnson had chosen her himself, picked her out from among the other candidates, overridden Gary Curst's objections. That was something she had been forced to get used to: Curst didn't like her. Or else he liked her too much. Perhaps he was jealous. Perhaps he was attracted to her. Whatever. He was certainly hostile toward her. Gratuitous hostility, everywhere, all the time, and there was nothing she could do about it.

Sarah knew plenty of ambitious men like him. Women-haters, men who felt threatened by their female colleagues. She paid them no attention. She trod her own path, left them by the wayside. She had stormed through the ranks at Johnson & Lockwood and established a fine reputation in court. The courtroom was her arena, her territory, her battleground. She would sweep in, ready for combat, intractable, merciless.

When she addressed the court, she used a subtly different voice, deeper, more solemn than her own. She spoke in short, incisive sentences, delivering knockout blows that left her adversaries reeling, sent them tumbling down the cracks in their arguments. She knew each case by heart. She was never caught off guard and never lost face. Since her earliest years in practice, with the small Winston Street firm that had taken her on straight out of law school, she had almost never lost a case. She was admired and feared. At forty years of age, she was the model of a successful, mid-career litigator.

In the firm, she was mooted as the next managing partner. Johnson was getting on in years now: a successor would have to be found. The partners were vying for position. They could see themselves already, taking the boss's place. Managing partner was the apotheosis, the Everest of any lawyer's career. Sarah ticked all the boxes: a spotless record, unshakable grit, an unrivaled capacity for hard work. Her insatiable appetite for work kept her moving ahead. She was an athlete, a mountaineer, conquering each new peak, never content to rest. Her life was a never-ending climb; sometimes, she wondered if she would ever reach the top. She waited for the day, but she didn't dare to hope.

Her career had demanded sacrifices, of course. It had claimed its share of sleepless nights, and both of her marriages. Sarah often said that men liked women who didn't put them in the shade, but she also admitted that two lawyers in a marriage was one too many. She had read a harsh statistic about lawyers' relationships in a women's magazine one day — not that she ever looked at them much. She had shown it to her then husband, and they had laughed — but separated a year later.

Work took up virtually all her time. Sarah had missed out on so many shared moments with her kids, passing up on school trips, end-of-year fetes, dance shows, birthday parties, holidays; and it cost her more than she cared to admit. She knew she could never get back all the moments she had missed, and the thought troubled her. She was no stranger to the working mom's guilt: it had plagued her ever since Hannah was born, since the dreadful day when she had been forced to leave her in the arms of a nanny, at five days old, and headed out to tackle an emergency at work. But she had very quickly understood there was no place, in her world, for the dramas and dilemmas of a heartbroken mother. She hid her tears under a thick coat of foundation and left for work. She felt torn apart, but there was no one in whom she could confide. She had envied her husband's cheerful, casual attitude. The fascinating insouciance of men, for whom guilt seemed not to exist. They stepped out the front door with appalling ease, taking nothing with them but their caseload, while she shouldered her burden of guilt, like a tortoise laboring under its shell. At first, she had tried to fight it, reject it, deny it, but she had never been able to. In the end, she had made a place for it in her life. Guilt was her longtime companion, the uninvited guest who accompanied her everywhere. The billboard passed in a field, a wart in the middle of a face: ugly and useless, but there it was. She dealt with it because she had to.

Sarah never let anything show to her colleagues and fellow partners. She made it a rule never to talk about her children. She didn't mention them, kept no pictures of them framed on her desk. If she had to leave work for a doctor's visit, or an unmissable appointment at school, she would say she had an "outside meeting." Better to say you were leaving early for "a quick drink" than because your nanny couldn't stay late. It was better to lie, to make things up and embroider the truth than to admit you had children. Children were synonymous with chains, ties, constraints. They compromised your availability, blocked your career path. Sarah remembered a woman at her old firm who had made partner, then announced she was pregnant, and found herself demoted, relegated to the lower ranks.

It was a kind of abuse. Mute, invisible abuse, a kind of everyday violence that no one dared to challenge. Sarah had learned her lesson: she had said nothing to her superiors about her two pregnancies. Amazingly, her bump was barely visible up until the seventh month, even for the twins, as if, deep inside her, the children sensed they had better keep out of sight. It was their little secret, a silent pact. Sarah had taken the shortest maternity leave possible, and returned to work two weeks after her caesarean, with a perfect figure and smile, flawlessly made up; underneath it all, though, her face was tired. Each morning, before pulling into her dedicated parking space at the foot of her office tower, she would stop at the parking lot of the nearby supermarket to take the two child seats from out of the back and put them in the trunk. Her colleagues knew she had children, of course, but she was careful not to remind them of the fact. The secretaries could chat about teething and the best baby food brands, but not a partner.

Sarah had built a wall between her professional and family lives. They ran on parallel tracks, never intersecting or overlapping. The wall was precarious and cracked in places; it threatened to topple over one day. But that didn't matter. She liked to think her children would be proud of what she had made, of what she was. She tried to make up for their lack of time together: quality, not quantity. In private, Sarah was a tender, attentive mother.

And for all the rest, there was Ron. "Magic Ron," to use the children's nickname. Which made him laugh. The name that had become almost an official title over time.

Sarah had hired Ron a few months before the twins' first birthday. She'd had trouble with Linda, the previous nanny, who was always late, and slack in her work, and who had eventually committed a gross error that prompted her immediate firing. One day, Sarah had hurried back home to fetch a file she had forgotten and found nine-month-old Ethan alone in his crib in a deserted house. An hour later, Linda had come back from the market with Simon, totally unconcerned. Caught red-handed, she had explained that she took the twins out separately, on alternate days, because taking them both out together was too difficult. Sarah had fired her on the spot. Pleading crippling sciatica at work, she had spent the next few days interviewing a succession of helps, including Ron. Surprised to find a male candidate, she had discounted him at first — too many stories in the papers. And her two husbands hadn't exactly distinguished themselves in the art of diaper-changing and bottle-feeding. She doubted another man would fare any better.

Then she remembered her own interview at Johnson & Lockwood, and all that she had had to accomplish, as a woman, in order to make a name for herself there. And so she reconsidered. Ron deserved a chance, like the others. Besides which, he had a great résumé and sound references. He had two children of his own. He lived in a nearby neighborhood. He had all the qualities required for the post. Sarah had given him a two-week trial, during which Ron had proved perfect for the job. He spent hours playing with the kids, his cooking was divine, he did the shopping, the cleaning, the washing, relieved her of every dull and exacting chore. The kids — Hannah, who was five at the time, and the twins — had all taken to him straightaway. Sarah had just left her second husband, the boys' father, and she felt a man around the house would be a good thing in a single-mom family like hers.

Subconsciously, perhaps, she was ensuring no woman would take her place. And so Ron had become Magic Ron, indispensable in their lives.

When she looked at herself in the mirror, Sarah saw a woman of forty who had it all: three beautiful children, a well-kept house in a smart neighborhood, a career that was the envy of many. She was the epitome of the women you read about in magazines: smiling, warm, accomplished. Her wound was invisible, almost undetectable. But look beyond her perfect makeup, her designer heels, and there it was.

Like thousands of women across the land, Sarah Cohen was split down the middle.

She was a bomb waiting to explode.

SMITA

Come here.
Wash yourself.
Don't hang about.

Today is the day. You cannot be late.

In the tiny yard behind the hut, Smita helps Lalita to wash. The little girl stands submissively, not even protesting when the water gets in her eyes. Smita untangles her daughter's waist-length hair. She has never cut it; here women keep their hair from birth, sometimes their whole lives. She divides the hair into three skeins, then braids them with expert hands. Then she holds out the sari she has stitched for Lalita, night after night. A neighbor gave her the fabric. She doesn't have the money for the school uniform, but that doesn't matter. Her daughter will look pretty on her first day, she tells herself.

She has been up since dawn, preparing her food — there are no meals in the little school. Each child brings their own. Smita has prepared rice and added a little of the curry powder she keeps for special occasions. She hopes Lalita will have some appetite on her first day. She will need energy to learn to read and write. In place of a *dabba,* she has put her daughter's rice in a carefully cleaned can, and she has even taken the trouble to decorate it. She doesn't want Lalita to be ashamed in front of the others. She will learn to read, just like them. Like the Jatt children.

Put on some powder. See to the altar. Hurry.

In the hut's only room — kitchen, bedroom, and temple — Lalita is in charge of the little altar to the gods. She lights a candle and places it beside the sacred images. It's her job to ring the bell when prayers are finished. Together, Smita and her daughter recite a prayer to Vishnu, the god of life and creation, protector of all humanity. When the order of the world is disrupted, he is made incarnate and comes down to Earth to set things straight, taking in turn the form of a fish, a turtle, a boar, a lion-man, even a man. Lalita likes to sit beside the small altar in the evening, after supper, and listen to her mother's stories of the ten avatars of Vishnu. During his first human incarnation, he defended the Brahmins against the Kshatriyas, and filled five lakes with their blood. Lalita shudders every time she hears the story. In her games, she is careful never to crush even the tiniest ant, the tiniest spider; you never know, Vishnu may be there, right beside you, incarnate as the lowest of creatures. A god at the tip of your finger. The idea delights her and terrifies her at the same time. Nagarajan enjoys listening to Smita, too, beside the altar in the evenings. His wife is a wonderful storyteller, though she has never learned how to read.

No time for stories this morning. Nagarajan has left early as usual, at first light. He is a rat catcher, like his father before him. He works in the Jatts' fields. It's an age-old tradition, a skill that is handed down, an inheritance of sorts: the art of catching rats with your bare hands. The rodents eat the crops and damage the soil with their tunnels. Nagarajan has learned to recognize the tiny, distinctive holes in the ground. You must be attentive, his father told him. And patient. Don't be afraid. You'll get bitten at first. You'll learn. He remembers his first catch, when he was eight years old, when he put his hand down the hole. A sharp pain tore through his flesh, like lightning: the rat had bitten the tender space between the thumb and forefinger, where the skin is soft and sensitive. Nagarajan had cried out and pulled his bloodstained hand free. His father had laughed. You're going about it the wrong way. You have to be quicker than that, take him by surprise. Try again. Nagarajan was frightened. He fought back his tears. Try again! He had tried again, six times, six bites, before pulling the huge rat from its hiding place. His father had grasped the animal by its tail and smashed its head against a stone, before handing it back to his son. There, he said, simply. Nagarajan had taken hold of the dead rat and carried it back home, like a trophy.

First, his mother had dressed his hand. Then she roasted the rat on the fire, and they had eaten it together for dinner.

Dalits like Nagarajan earn no wages, they are merely allowed to keep what they catch. A privilege, of a kind: the rats are the property of the Jatts, like the fields and whatever is in them or lies beneath them. It's not bad, grilled. Some say it tastes a little like chicken. The poor man's chicken. The Dalits' chicken. The only meat they have. Nagarajan tells how his father ate rats whole, with their skin and fur, leaving only the indigestible tail. He would skewer the animal on a stick, grill it over the fire, then crunch it whole. Lalita laughs whenever she hears the story. Smita prefers to skin the rats first. In the evening, they eat that day's rats with rice, from which Smita keeps the cooking water, to use as a sauce. Sometimes, the families whose latrines she empties also give her their leftovers. She brings them home and shares them with the neighbors.

Your bindi.
Don't forget.

Lalita searches through her things and takes out a small bottle of nail polish she found one day when she was playing by the side of a path. A lady had dropped her bag, and the bottle had fallen out. Lalita didn't dare tell her mother she had taken it. The bottle had rolled into the ditch, and the child had retrieved it, clutching it tight like a piece of treasure and keeping it hidden from sight. She had brought the booty home that evening and pretended she had found it. Her heart had swelled with joy, and with shame. What if Vishnu knew . . .

Smita takes the bottle from her daughter and draws a bright scarlet spot on her forehead. The circle must be perfect, it's a delicate technique, it takes practice. She taps the polish gently with the tip of her finger, then fixes it with powder. The bindi, the "third eye," retains energy and enhances one's concentration. Lalita will need it today, Smita tells herself. She looks at the small, evenly shaped circle on her daughter's forehead, and smiles. Lalita is pretty. She has regular features, dark eyes. Her mouth has the delicate outline of a petal. She is lovely in her green sari. Smita is filled with pride at the sight of her daughter, the schoolgirl. She may eat rat meat, but she will learn how to read, she thinks to herself, as she takes Lalita by the hand and leads her to the main road. She will help her. The trucks thunder past from early in the morning and there are no traffic lights, nowhere safe to cross.

Lalita looks up anxiously at her mother as they walk: she's not frightened of the trucks, but of this new world, completely unknown to her parents, which she must enter alone. Smita senses the little girl's imploring look; it would be so easy to turn around, pick up the rush basket and take her along with her . . . But no, she will not see Lalita vomit into the ditch. Her daughter will go to school. She will learn how to read, write, and do arithmetic.

Do your best.
Do as you're told.
Listen to the teacher.

The little girl looks suddenly lost, and so fragile that Smita wants to take her in her arms and never let her go. She must fight the urge, however hard it hurts. The teacher had said "yes" when Nagarajan went to see him. He had seen the box into which Smita had put all their savings — coins carefully set aside for months on end for Lalita's schooling. He had taken it and said, "All right." Smita knows that's how everything works. Money has the power of persuasion. Nagarajan had come home to announce the good news to his wife and daughter, and they had all rejoiced.

They cross and suddenly it is upon them, the moment when she must let go of her daughter's hand on the other side of the road. There is so much Smita wants to say: be happy, you won't have my life, you'll have good health, you won't cough like me, you'll live longer and better than I have, you'll have respect. You won't carry the foul smell, the cursed, indelible scent. You'll have dignity. No one will throw their scraps to you, like a dog. You will not lower your head, or your eyes. Smita badly wants to tell her all this. But she's not sure how to say it, how to tell her daughter about her wild hopes and dreams, about the butterflies fluttering in her stomach.

So she bends over her, and says simply: "Go."

GIULIA

Palermo, Sicily

Giulia woke with a start.

She had dreamed of her father in the night. As a child, she used to love going with him on his rounds. They would set off together on his Vespa, early in the morning. She never rode behind, but in front, on her father's knees. She loved the wind in her hair, the dizzying sensation of infinite space and freedom that comes when you travel at speed. She was never afraid, her father's arm was tight around her waist, she was completely safe. She cried out in joy and excitement when they hurtled downhill. She saw the sun rise over the Sicilian coast, the early-morning bustle of the neighborhoods, life waking up and stretching to greet the new day.

More than anything, she loved knocking at people's doors. "Good morning! It's for the *cascatura*," she would announce

51

proudly. Sometimes, the women would give her a piece of candy or a picture postcard along with their sachets of hair.

Giulia would proudly collect the booty and hand it to her father. He would reach into his bag and take out the small set of cast-iron scales he carried everywhere, handed down from his father, and his father before him. He would weigh the strands, estimate their value, and present the women with a few coins. In the past, they had exchanged their hair for matches, but when cigarette lighters came in, the trade soon died out. Now the women were paid in cash.

Often, her father would chuckle at the old people, who were too weak to come down from their bedrooms but would still drop down a basket of their hair on a rope. He would wave, take the strands, and put the money in the basket, ready to be pulled back up.

Giulia remembered that: how her father laughed when he told her about it.

Then they would set off for the next houses on their list. *Arrivederci!* At the hair salons, the spoils were even greater, and Giulia loved her father's expression when he received a long skein of hair, the rarest and most valuable. He would weigh it, measure it, feel the strands' texture and thickness. He would pay up, thank the client, and leave. There was no time to lose. The Lanfredi workshop had a hundred suppliers in Palermo alone. If they hurried, they could be back in time for lunch.

The image held a moment longer: Giulia at nine years old, riding aboard the Vespa.

The seconds that followed were vague, confused, as if reality itself was struggling to focus, caught up in the dream that had just ended.

So it was true. Her father had had an accident the day before, on his rounds. For some unknown reason, his Vespa had skidded off the road. And yet he knew the route well, had ridden it hundreds of times. Perhaps an animal ran out in front of him, the paramedics had suggested. Or perhaps he'd suffered a stroke. No one knew. Now he was in Francesco Saverio Hospital, hovering between life and death. The doctors were saying nothing. You must be prepared for the worst, they had told her mamma.

The worst. Giulia couldn't contemplate that. Fathers didn't die. Fathers lived forever. A rock, a pillar, especially hers. Pietro Lanfredi was a force of nature, he would live to be a hundred, as his friend Dr. Signore liked to tell him over a glass of grappa. Pietro, the lover of good food and wine, and good company, her papà, the patriarch, the boss, with his fiery temper and his passion for life, her father, her adored father. He couldn't leave. Not now, not like this.

Today was the Feast of Santa Rosalia, thought Giulia, with grim irony. Palermo was celebrating its patron saint. The *festinu* would go on all day, as it did every year. And like every year, her father had given the workers the day off so that they could take part in the festivities: the procession along the Corso Vittorio Emanuele, and the fireworks at nightfall on the Foro Italico.

Giulia was in no mood to celebrate. She had made her way to her father's bedside with her mother and sisters and tried to ignore the festivities outside in the streets. Lying in the hospital bed, he showed no sign of suffering, which was some comfort to her. His once-robust form looked so fragile now; he might almost be a child. He seemed smaller than before, as if he had shrunk. Maybe that's what happens when the soul slips away. She chased the morbid thought from her mind. Her father was there. He was still alive. They must cling to that. Head trauma, the doctors said. Which meant: we don't know. No one could say whether he would live or die. It seemed his own mind wasn't made up, either.

We must pray, Mamma had insisted. That morning, she had asked Giulia and her sisters to walk in the procession for Santa Rosalia. The flower-decked Virgin performed miracles, she said. She had proved her power in the past when she saved the city from the plague: we must call upon her to intercede. Giulia disliked these displays of religious fervor, with their dense, excitable, unpredictable crowds. Besides, she didn't believe any of it. She had been baptized, of course, and made her communion — she remembered wearing the traditional white dress and receiving the Holy Sacrament for the first time under the intense, pious gaze of her assembled family. The memory was one of the happiest of her life. But today, she felt no desire to pray. She wanted to stay at her papà's side.

Her mother had insisted. If the doctors were powerless, God alone could save him. Her conviction was such that Giulia felt suddenly envious of her mother's faith — the unshakable faith that had never deserted her. Her mother was the most pious woman she knew. She went to church every week, to hear the Latin mass, of which she understood barely a word. There was no need to understand in order to worship God, as she liked to say. Finally, Giulia had given in.

Together, they had joined the procession and the crowds of Santa Rosalia's admirers lining the route between the cathedral and the Quattro Canti. An ocean of humanity, packed tight to pay tribute to the Virgin of the Flowers, whose gigantic statue was borne through the streets. July was hot in Palermo, the air was stifling. In the midst of the procession, Giulia found it hard to breathe. She heard a ringing in her ears; her vision clouded.

Her mother stopped to greet a neighbor who was asking after Papà — the news had spread fast — and Giulia seized her moment to slip away. She took refuge in a shady side street and drank some water from a fountain. The air was clearer, she could breathe again. Her spirits revived. Voices rang out farther along the street. Two uniformed *carabinieri* were issuing a warning to a tall, well-built, dark-skinned man, his hair covered by a turban, which the two police officers were ordering him to remove. The man protested, in perfect Italian with a hint of a foreign accent. Everything's in order, he told them, showing his papers. But the officers would not listen. They became angry and threatened to take him to the cells if he still refused to comply. He might have a weapon concealed in his headgear, they said. Nothing could be left to chance on the day of the procession. The man stood his ground. The turban was a sign of his religious allegiance; he was forbidden to remove it in public. And it did not prevent him from being identified, he continued, because he was wearing it in his ID photograph — a privilege granted to Sikhs by the Italian government. Giulia watched the scene and felt uncomfortable. The man was good-looking, with an athletic figure, fine features, and curiously pale eyes. He looked about thirty years old at most. The *carabinieri* grew angrier still. One of them pushed the man. Then, holding him firmly between them, they led him away, in the direction of the police station.

The unknown man showed no resistance. He passed in front of Giulia with a dignified, resigned air, flanked by the two *carabinieri.* For an instant, their eyes met. Giulia did not lower her gaze, and neither did the stranger. She watched as he disappeared around the corner at the end of the street.

"Che fai?!"

Francesca had appeared behind her, making her jump.

"We've been looking for you everywhere.

Andiamo! Dai!"

Regretfully, Giulia rejoined the procession, walking behind her sister.

That evening, she found it hard to get to sleep. The image of the dark-skinned man returned. She couldn't help wondering what had happened to him, what the police officers had done. Had he been interrogated? Beaten? Sent for deportation to his own country? She was lost in pointless speculation. One question tormented her above all: Should she have intervened? And what could she have done? She felt guilty at her passive response. She had no idea why the stranger's fate intrigued her so. She had felt a strange, unfamiliar sensation when she looked at him. Was it curiosity? Empathy?

Or something else, something she could not name.

SARAH

Montreal, Canada

Sarah had just collapsed. In court, in the middle of a plea. She had found herself short of breath, faltered in her speech, and then stared around her as if, all of a sudden, she had no idea where she was. She had tried to pick up the thread of her argument, despite her white complexion and trembling hands — the only sign that anything was wrong. Then her vision had clouded and darkened as the room closed in around her. Her heartbeat had slowed, and the blood had drained from her face, like a river shifting its course. She had collapsed to the floor, right where she stood, like the supposedly unshakable Twin Towers of the World Trade Center. She fell in complete silence. She had not called out in protest, or for help. She just sank to the ground, making no noise, like a house of cards, quite gracefully, in fact.

When she opened her eyes, a man was bending over her, wearing a paramedic's uniform.

"You passed out, madam. We're taking you to the hospital."

The man had called her "madam." Sarah was just regaining consciousness, but the form of address didn't escape her. She hated being called "madam." The term was a slap in the face to every woman of a certain age. Sarah hated the word, which seemed to say, "You're not a girl, or a young woman anymore, you've moved on to the next category." She hated forms and questionnaires that insisted she tick the box corresponding to her age. She had been forced to abandon the seductive 30–39 age group for the less attractive 40–49. Fortysomething. Sarah hadn't seen that coming. She had been just fine at thirty-eight, even thirty-nine, but not forty, no, she really hadn't been expecting that. She hadn't thought it would come so quickly. "No one is young after forty . . ." She remembered reading Coco Chanel's phrase in a magazine and closing it right away. She hadn't taken the time to read the rest: ". . . but a person can be irresistible at any age."

Miss. Sarah corrected the man immediately as she sat up. She tried to get to her feet, but the paramedic stopped her with a gentle but commanding gesture. She protested — she was in the middle of pleading a case. An urgent and highly important case, as they always were.

"You cut yourself when you fell. You're going to need stitches."

Inès was standing beside her, the colleague she had recruited, who assisted her with her caseload. The session had been adjourned, she told her. She had just called the office to postpone her upcoming meetings. Inès was efficient and quick off the mark, as always. In a word, perfect. She seemed concerned about Sarah, offered to come with her to the hospital. But Sarah told her she had better get back to the office, she could be of more use there. She could get on with preparing tomorrow's assignment.

Sarah sat waiting in the emergency room at CHUM. Montreal's university hospital did not live up to its charming acronym, she thought. In Canada, the word meant a boyfriend, a lover. But there was nothing to seduce her here. Eventually, she rose to leave; she had no intention of spending two hours waiting for three stitches to her forehead when a Band-Aid would do the job. She had to get back to work. A doctor caught her by the arm and escorted her back to her seat. She must wait to be examined. Sarah protested, but had no choice other than to comply.

The intern who examined her, at last, had long, delicate hands and an air of concentration. He asked her a great many questions, to which Sarah gave brief, laconic answers. She couldn't see the point of all this, she was fine, she kept telling him, but the intern persisted with his examination. Against her better judgment, like a criminal suspect delivering a hard-won confession, she admitted that yes, she had been feeling tired lately. How could she not feel tired when she had three children, a house to keep, a fridge to fill, and a full-time job?

Sarah didn't tell him that she had woken up exhausted every morning for the past month. That every evening, when she got home, after listening to Ron's report of his day with the kids, after dinner with them, after putting the twins to bed, after helping Hannah with her homework, she would collapse onto the sitting room sofa and fall asleep before she had time to reach for the remote and switch on the giant flat-screen TV she had just bought, but never watched.

She didn't tell him about the pain in her chest, on the left side, that she had felt from time to time, for a while now. Probably nothing . . . She didn't want to talk about it, not there, not now, not to this stranger in a white coat, with his cold, penetrating stare. Now was not the time.

But the intern seemed concerned. Sarah's blood pressure was low, and she was dreadfully pale. Sarah made light of it. She was pretending, putting him off the scent. She was good at that; it was her job, after all. Everyone at the office knew the old joke: How can you tell when a lawyer is lying? You can see their lips move. She had got the better of some of the wiliest magistrates in town; this young intern wouldn't catch her out. A minor blip, was all. Burnout? She smiled at the term. The expression was very current, and very overused, too. A big word for a passing bout of fatigue. She hadn't eaten enough this morning, that was all. Or maybe she hadn't slept enough? Hadn't screwed enough, either, she was tempted to add, with wry humor, but the intern's severe expression dissuaded her from any attempt to get to know him a little better. A shame. He was almost good-looking, with his little glasses and curly hair, almost her type. She would take vitamins, if he wanted, yes. She could recommend a terrific pick-me-up, she told him, smiling: coffee, cocaine, and cognac. Highly effective, he should try it some time.

The intern was in no mood for jokes. He suggested rest, a break from work. "Take your foot off the accelerator," he said. Sarah burst out laughing. So he did have a sense of humor after all. Take her foot off the accelerator? How exactly? By selling the kids on eBay? By declaring that, as of tonight, they were giving up food? By announcing to her clients that she was going on strike? She was handling a number of highly important cases, which were impossible to delegate. Stopping was not an option. She'd forgotten the meaning of the term "take a break." She could hardly even remember the last time she took a holiday. Last year? Or the year before? The intern muttered something she chose to ignore: No one is irreplaceable. Clearly, he had no idea what it meant to be a partner at Johnson & Lockwood. No idea what it meant to be in Sarah Cohen's shoes.

She wanted to go, now. The intern tried to persuade her to stay for more tests, but she talked her way out of them, though it was unlike her to put something off until the next day. At school, she had been a star pupil, "very studious," her teachers had said. She hated doing a piece of work at the last minute. She liked to "get a head start," as she put it, and had always devoted the first few hours of each weekend, or the school breaks, to her homework, so that she felt freer afterward. It was the same at work: she always had a head start over the others, that's what had enabled her to rise so fast. She left nothing to chance. *She always planned ahead.*

But not here. Not now. Now was not the time.

And so Sarah headed back to her world, to her appointments, her conference calls, her lists, her cases, her pleas, her meetings, her notes, her minutes, her business lunches, her assignments, her referrals, her three children. She headed back to the front like a good recruit, donned the mask she always wore, the one that suited her so well, the mask of the smiling, successful super-woman. The mask was intact. Not so much as a hairline crack. Back at work, she would reassure Inès and her colleagues: it was nothing. And everything would carry on as before.

In the weeks ahead, there would be a checkup with her gynecologist. Yes, I feel something, she would say, while checking Sarah's breasts, and her expression would be tinged with worry. She would prescribe a series of tests with outlandish names that strike fear whenever they're spoken: mammogram, scan, biopsy. The tests that are practically a diagnosis in themselves. A pronouncement of sentence.

But now was not the time for all that. Against the intern's advice, Sarah left the hospital.

For the moment, everything was fine.

If you didn't talk about it, it didn't exist.

A space no bigger than a bedroom.
You could fit a bed inside, at most,
And even then, only a child's bed.
This is where I work, alone,
Day after day, in silence.

There are machines for this,
Of course,
But the result is less fine.
No production line here.
Each model is unique.
And each one makes me proud.

Over time, my hands have learned their
    work,
Independent of my body.
The gesture is taught.
But speed comes with years of practice.

I've been working for so long, bent over
    my loom,

That my eyes are strained.

My body is tired,
Stiff with rheumatism,
Yet my fingers have lost none of their
    agility.

Sometimes my mind floats
Far away from the workshop,
Transporting me to distant countries
And lives unknown,
Whose voices reach me here,
Like a faint echo,
And intertwine with my own.

SMITA

Badlapur, Uttar Pradesh, India

Smita enters the hut. Right away, she sees the expression on her daughter's face.

She had hurried to finish her rounds and didn't call on her neighbor to share the Jatts' leftovers, as she usually did. She had run to the well to fetch water, set down her rush basket, and washed herself in the yard — one bucket, no more, leaving enough for Lalita and Nagarajan.

Each evening, before stepping over the threshold of her house, Smita rubs her body all over three times with soap. She refuses to bring that vile stench home; she doesn't want her husband and daughter to associate her with the filthy smell. That smell, the smell of other people's shit, is not her; she will not allow herself to be reduced to that. And so she scrubs her hands, her feet, her body, her face with all her strength, she scrubs enough to rub away her skin, behind the piece of cloth that serves as a screen at the far end of the yard on the edge of the village in Badlapur, in a far-flung corner of Uttar Pradesh.

Smita dries herself and puts on clean clothes before entering the hut. Lalita is sitting in a corner, her knees folded tight against her chest. She is staring at the ground. An expression flickers over her face, one that her mother has never seen before, an indefinable mixture of anger and sadness. She moves closer.

"What is the matter?"

The child says nothing. Her jaw is clenched tight.

"Tell me."

"How was your day?"

"Say something!"

Lalita says nothing and stares into space, as if fixing her gaze upon an imaginary point that only she can see, an inaccessible place, far from the hut, far from the village, where no one can reach her, not even her mother. Smita is angry now.

"Speak!"

Lalita curls tighter into herself, like a frightened snail retreating inside its shell. It would be so easy to shake her, to shout, to force her to speak. But Smita knows her daughter: she will get nothing out of her that way. The butterflies in her stomach are a crab now. She is gripped by a feeling of anguish. What happened at school? She knew nothing of that world, and yet she sent her daughter there, her treasure. Had she been wrong? What had they done to her?

She looks carefully at the child, then stands rooted to the spot: her sari seems to have been ripped at the back. Yes, it is torn!

"What have you done?"
"You've got yourself dirty!"
"Wherever have you been?!"

Smita catches hold of Lalita's hand and pulls her daughter toward her, peeling her from the wall. The new sari, the sari she had stitched, night after night, for hours, losing sleep so that it would be ready in time, the sari that was her pride and joy, is ripped and ruined and filthy!

"You've torn it! Look!"

Smita begins to shout. She is furious. And then she stops dead. A terrible thought has struck her. She takes Lalita outside into the yard, into the light — the interior of the hut is dark; hardly any daylight enters. She sets about undressing her, pulling roughly at the sari. Lalita shows no resistance. The fabric comes away easily. Smita stops. She can see

71

Lalita's back: it is streaked with red lines. The marks of the cane. Her skin has split in places, raw and red. Scarlet, like her bindi.

"Who did this to you? Tell me! Who hit you?"
The little girl lowers her eyes. Two words escape.
"The schoolteacher."

Smita's face is dark red. The vein in her neck is swollen with anger — Lalita is terrified by the small, bulging vein. It frightens her.

Her mother is usually so calm. Smita catches hold of the child and shakes her. Her small, naked body trembles like a twig.

"Why? What did you do? Did you disobey?!"

Smita explodes with rage: her daughter has been disobedient, on the very first day of school! The teacher will not take her back, for sure, all her hopes have vanished, all her effort for nothing! She knows what this means: the latrines, the slime, other people's shit. The basket, that cursed basket from which she had so wanted to save her.

Smita has never shown violence, she has never hit another person, but suddenly she feels an uncontrollable burst of rage. A new

72

sensation that fills her whole body, a tide that breaches the dam of reason and engulfs her. She slaps the child. Lalita huddles against the blows, she protects her face with her hands, as best she can.

Nagarajan is on his way home from the fields when he hears the cries from the yard. He hurries back. He places himself between his wife and his daughter.

"Smita! Stop!"

He manages to push her away and takes the child in his arms. She is racked with sobs. He discovers the marks on her back, the stripes, and the split skin. He holds her tight against him.

She has disobeyed the Brahmin, yells Smita. Nagarajan looks into his daughter's face, holding her still.

"Is this true?"

After a moment's silence, Lalita mumbles a phrase that stings them both like a sharp slap.

"He wanted me to sweep the classroom."

Smita stands frozen. Lalita spoke the words so low, she isn't even sure she heard them correctly.

"What did you say?" she whispers.

"He wanted me to sweep up, in front of the others. I said no."

Fearing she will be hit again, the child

73

curls up tight. She seems smaller, as if shrunk by fear. Smita cannot breathe. She draws her daughter to her, holds her as tight as her frail limbs will allow, and begins to cry. The little girl buries her face in her mother's neck; she has let go, they have made their peace. They stay like that for a long time, under Nagarajan's bewildered gaze. He has never seen his wife cry before. In the face of all the trials life has sent her way, she has never flinched, never broken. She is a strong, determined woman. But not today. Clinging tight to her daughter's hurt, humiliated body, she is a child once more, like Lalita, and she weeps for her dashed hopes, for the life she had so long dreamed of and which she cannot give her now, because there will always be Jatts and Brahmins to remind them who they are, and where they come from.

In the evening, when they have put Lalita to bed and lulled her to sleep at last, Smita unleashes her fury. Why did he do that? That teacher, that Brahmin? He had agreed to take Lalita with the others, the Jatt children, he had taken their money and said "All right!" Smita knows him, that man, and his family, too. His house is in the center of the village. She cleans their latrines every day. His wife gives her rice sometimes. So why?

Suddenly she thinks of the five lakes that Vishnu filled with the blood of the Kshatriyas while defending the Brahmin caste: the educated people, the priests, the enlightened ones, above all the other castes, the summit of all humanity. Why attack Lalita? Her daughter was no danger to them, no threat to their learning, nor their status, so why push her back down into the slime? Why not teach her to read and write, like the other children?

Sweeping the classroom means: You have no right to be here. You are a Dalit, a *scavenger,* and a scavenger you will remain, your whole life long. You will die in other people's shit, like your mother and your grandmother before you. Like your children, and your grandchildren, and all your progeny. There will be nothing else for you, the untouchables, the rejects of humanity, nothing but that vile stench, for hundreds and hundreds of years, just other people's shit. The shit of the entire human race.

Lalita had not given in. She had said no. Smita feels proud of her daughter. This six-year-old child, barely taller than the stool the schoolteacher sat on, had looked the Brahmin in the eyes and said, "No." He had caught hold of her and caned her in the middle of the class, in front of all the oth-

75

ers. Lalita hadn't cried, hadn't shouted out, she hadn't made a sound. The bell had rung for the midday break. The Brahmin had denied Lalita her meal; he had confiscated the little metal tin that Smita had prepared for her. The little girl was not even allowed to sit, only to watch the others eat. She had not protested, not begged. She had stood alone, and dignified. Yes, Smita is proud of her daughter. She may eat rat meat, but she is stronger than all the Brahmins and the Jatts put together. They will not tame her, they will never break her spirit. They had struck with the cane, striped her back with scars, but she was still there. Self-possessed. Intact.

Nagarajan does not agree with his wife: Lalita should have given in, taken the broom, that's not such a bad thing to have to do, a few swishes of the broom — less painful than the swishes of the cane . . .

Smita explodes. How can he say such a thing? School is where children go to learn, not sweep the floors. She'll go and talk to him, that Brahmin, she knows where he lives, she knows the hidden door at the back of his house, she goes in that way every day with her rush basket to clean out his filth . . . Nagarajan stops her: there is nothing to be gained by confronting the Brahmin. He is so much more powerful than her. Everyone is more powerful than her. Lalita must accept the bullying, if she wants to go back to school. It's the price she must pay if she is to learn to read and write. That's how it is in this world. You can't break out of your caste and go unpunished.

Smita glares at her husband. She is trembling with rage. She will not let her child become the Brahmin's scapegoat. How could Nagarajan even think such a thing? He should be defending her, making a stand, fighting for his daughter against the whole world.

"Isn't that what a father does?"

Smita would rather die than send Lalita back to school; Lalita will not set foot there again. Smita curses a society that crushes its weakest members, its women, its children, the very people it should protect.

Nagarajan agrees. Lalita will not go back there tomorrow. Smita will take her along on her rounds, he says. She will teach her the trade practiced by her mother, and her grandmother before her. She will give her the basket. After all, it's what the women of her family have done for centuries. It is her dharma. Smita was wrong to have hoped for anything else. She had wanted to set Lalita on another path, a different path from the one laid out for her. And the Brahmin had beaten her back into place with his cane.

The discussion is closed.

That night, Smita prays before the little altar to Vishnu. She knows she won't be able to sleep. She thinks again about the five lakes of blood and wonders, How many lakes must be filled with *their* blood, the blood of the untouchables, to free them from the yoke they have carried for thousands of years? There were millions like her. Multitudes resigned to their fate, waiting patiently for death. Everything will be better in the next life, her mother used to say. And perhaps the relentless cycle of reincarnation will be broken. Nirvana, the ultimate destination, that was what she hoped for. She dreamed of dying beside the Ganges, the sacred river. After that, it was said, the harsh grind of life would cease. Never to be reborn — to melt into the absolute, the cosmos, that was the ultimate goal. A blessing not granted to many, her mother said. Most were condemned to live. We must accept the order of things as a divine punishment. That's how it is: eternity must be earned.

And while they wait for eternity, the Dalits cower, and work.

But not Smita. Not this day.

She has accepted the cruel inevitability of her lot. But they will not have her daughter. She promises herself this, in front of the altar to Vishnu, in the dark hut where her husband is already sleeping. No, they will not have Lalita. Her rebellion is silent, inaudible, almost invisible.

But it is there.

GIULIA

Palermo, Sicily

He's like Sleeping Beauty, thought Giulia, as she looked at her father.

He had been lying between the white sheets of the hospital bed for eight days now. His condition was stable. He looked peaceful, sleeping like a bride who waits to be awoken. Giulia remembered the story of the *Bella Addormentata* that he would read to her when she was a child. He would put on a deeper voice for the Wicked Fairy, the one who casts the evil spell. She had heard the story a thousand times, but it was always a relief when the princess awoke at last. She had loved that so much: her father's voice ringing through the house at bedtime.

The voice was silent now.
Everything was silent now, around her
papà's bed.

■ ■ ■ ■

They had gone back to work — what else was there to do? The women had all shown Giulia their support. Gina had cooked her the *cassate* she loved so much. Agnese had bought chocolates for Mamma. La Nonna had offered to take turns at Papà's bedside. Alessia, whose brother was a priest, had offered prayers to Santa Caterina. Giulia was surrounded by a small, close-knit community that refused to succumb to grief. For their sake, she wanted to remain positive, just like her father. He would wake from the coma, she was certain of that. He would take his place at the helm of the workshop once again. This was just an interlude, she told herself, a moment suspended in time.

She sat at his bedside every evening, after the workshop had closed for the night. She had taken to reading aloud to him. According to the doctors, coma patients could hear what was being said around them. And so Giulia read aloud, for hours: poetry, prose, novels. My turn to read him stories now, she thought. He who read so much to me. Her papà could hear her, from where he lay, she knew that.

She had gone to the library today on her lunch break to borrow books for him. And a curious thing happened when she stepped into the reading room, bathed in silence. At first, she didn't notice it, hidden between the bookstacks. Suddenly she saw it.

There it was.
The turban.
The turban she had seen before, out in the street, on the Feast of Santa Rosalia.

Giulia was dumbfounded. The stranger was standing with his back to her. She couldn't see his face. He moved to another row. She followed him, intrigued. When he reached for a book, she saw his face at last. It really was him, the man who had been arrested by the *carabinieri.* He seemed to be looking for something, but unable to find it. Struck by the coincidence, Giulia watched him for a moment. He hadn't seen her.

Finally, she approached him. She had no idea what to say — she wasn't in the habit of talking to men she didn't know. As a rule, they were the ones who came to flirt with her. Giulia was beautiful, people often told her so. Despite her tomboy looks, there was an innocence about her, coupled with a sensuality that seldom left men indifferent. She felt their eyes on her as she passed by. Italian males were skilled talkers. Fine words, the usual overtures, she knew where it could lead. But she was surprised by her own audacity today.

"Buongiorno."

The stranger turned, in surprise. He didn't seem to recognize her. Giulia hesitated, awkwardly.

"I saw you the other day, in the street, during the procession. When the police . . ."

She paused. She was embarrassed now. What if it upset him to be reminded of the incident? She regretted being so forward. She wanted to disappear, she wished she had never approached him. But the man had recognized her now. He nodded. Giulia went on:

"I was afraid . . . they'd put you in prison."

The man smiled, and his expression was frank and amused. Who was this strange girl who seemed so worried about him?

"They kept me in for the afternoon, and then they let me go."

Giulia studied his face. His skin was dark, but his eyes were astonishingly pale. She could see them clearly now. They were blue, bordering on green — or perhaps the opposite. An intriguing mixture. She felt emboldened.

"I can help you. I know all these shelves. Are you looking for something in particular?"

The man said he wanted to read a book in Italian. Nothing too complicated, he told her. He spoke the language fluently, but he still had trouble with the written word. He wanted to improve. Giulia nodded. She took him to the Italian literature section. She hesitated — the contemporary authors were difficult, inaccessible, she thought. Finally, she recommended a novel by Salgari that she had read as a child: *I figli dell'aria,* her favorite. The man took it and thanked her. Any Sicilian man would try to keep her from leaving, engage her in conversation, take advantage of the moment to try to seduce her. Not him. He simply wished her a pleasant afternoon and walked away.

Giulia watched as he left the library, armed with the book he had just borrowed. She felt something tighten around her heart and regretted not having the courage to go after him. Such things weren't done here. No one ran after a man they had just met. Regretfully, Giulia knew she was still that young girl who leans on her elbows to watch every passing event but does nothing to alter their course. She cursed herself there and then, for her shyness, her passive nature.

Of course there had been boyfriends, flirtations, romantic encounters. Stolen kisses and caresses. Giulia had gone along with them, responding to the show of interest. But she had never gone out of her way to attract men.

She returned to the workshop, thinking about the stranger with his turban, which made him look out of place, out of time. She thought about the hair it concealed. And his body, too, beneath the crumpled shirt. At that thought, she blushed.

She went back to the library the next day, secretly hoping to meet him again. She didn't need any more books; she hadn't finished the ones she was reading to Papà. She entered the reading room and froze. There he was. In the same spot as the day before. He lifted his eyes to her, as if he had been waiting. At that moment, Giulia felt her heart leap.

He came over to her, standing so close she could feel his warm, sweet breath. He wanted to thank her for the book she had recommended. He didn't know what to offer her in return, and so he had brought a small bottle of olive oil from the cooperative where he worked. Giulia was touched. She looked at him, saw a mixture of gentleness and dignity that moved her deeply. It was the first time a man had made her feel that way.

She took the little bottle in surprise. He told her he had gathered and pressed the olives himself. He was preparing to leave, but Giulia stopped him. She felt quite brazen now. Perhaps they could take a walk together? The sea was close by, the sky was clear . . .

The stranger hesitated, then agreed.

His name was Kamaljit Singh. He was very quiet — which surprised Giulia. Sicilian men were talkative, they enjoyed making conversation with one another. The woman's role was to listen, as her mother had told her. The man must be allowed to shine. Kamal was different. He didn't open up easily. But he agreed to tell Giulia his story.

He was a Sikh. He had left Kashmir at the age of twenty, fleeing the violence against his people. After the events of 1984, when the Indian army had crushed a Sikh independence movement and massacred the faithful in the Golden Temple, their fate had been sealed. Kamal had arrived in Sicily one night, in the icy cold, without his parents. Many chose to send their children to the West once they came of age. He had been welcomed into the island's large Sikh community.

Italy had taken in the second largest number of Sikhs in Europe, after Great Britain, he said. He had found work through the *caporalato,* the traditional system for hiring cheap labor. He told her how the *caporale* recruited undocumented workers and arranged their transport. The gangmaster covered the cost of this, and the bottled water and meager *panino* he provided for his workers, by taking a percentage of their earnings, sometimes as much as half. Kamal remembered working for one or two euros an hour. He had picked everything that grew on the island: lemons, olives, cherry tomatoes, oranges, artichokes, zucchini, almonds. The pickers' working conditions were nonnegotiable. They could take what the *caporale* offered or leave it. His patience had finally been rewarded: after three years as an illegal immigrant, Kamal had obtained refugee status and a permanent residence permit. He had found a job working nights for a cooperative that produced olive oil. He enjoyed the work. He described how he combed the branches of the olive trees with a kind of rake to pull down the fruit. He liked the company of the trees: some were over a thousand years old.

He was fascinated by their longevity, he said. The olive is a noble foodstuff, he concluded, smiling. A symbol of peace.

The authorities had given him his papers, but the country had not adopted him as its own. Sicilian society eyed the immigrant population warily, from a distance. The two worlds seldom mixed. Kamal missed his home country, he said. When he talked about it, a great veil of sadness seemed to wrap itself around him, like a cloak.

Giulia came back to the workshop two hours late that day. She reassured her anxious Nonna by telling her that her bicycle had suffered a puncture.

She kept the truth to herself: her bike was intact, but her soul had veered wildly off course.

SARAH

Montreal, Canada
The bomb had detonated, right there in the office of an awkward doctor who had no idea how to tell her the news. He had plenty of experience, years of practice, but there it was — he could never get used to it. Too much empathy with his patients, no doubt, all the young and not-so-young women who saw their lives change forever in just a few moments, when the dreaded diagnosis was delivered.

BRCA2. Sarah would learn the name of the mutant gene soon enough. The curse of Ashkenazi women. As if they hadn't suffered enough, she would say. The pogroms, the Shoah . . . Why this, now, for her and her people?

She saw it spelled out in black and white in a medical article: Ashkenazi Jewish women have a one-in-forty chance of developing breast cancer, compared with one in five hundred in the world's population as a whole. It was a scientifically established fact. There were other aggravating factors: a previous history of cancer in the immediate family, falling pregnant with twins . . . All the signs were there, thought Sarah. Plain to see, obvious. But she hadn't seen them. Or hadn't wanted to see them.

The doctor sat opposite her. He had dark, bushy eyebrows. Sarah was transfixed by them. How strange: this man she didn't know was talking to her about the tumor on her X-rays — the size of a mandarin, he said — and yet she was unable to concentrate on his words. All she could see, it seemed, were his brown, bushy eyebrows, like heathland, populated with wild beasts. There was hair coming out of his ears, too. Astonishingly, months later, when Sarah thought about that day, that was the memory that came to her first: the eyebrows of the doctor who had told her she had cancer.

He didn't say the actual word, of course; no one spoke the word, you had to spot it, lurking behind all the euphemisms, the paraphrases, the deluge of medical jargon. As if it was some kind of insult, a taboo, a curse. And that was exactly what it was.

The size of a mandarin orange, he said. It's there. It's really there. And yet Sarah had done everything to put off the inevitable, to ignore the nagging pain, the extreme tiredness. She had pushed the idea from her mind whenever it occurred; whenever she could — or should — have put it into words. But she had to face it now. It was there. It was real.

A mandarin was huge and insignificant at the same time, she thought. The disease had taken her by surprise, just when she least expected it. The tumor was malignant, devious, it had gone about its work silently, in the shadows, preparing to strike.

Sarah listened to the doctor, watched his lips move, but his words seemed incapable of reaching her, as if she heard them through a thick, soft blanket, as if they weren't really anything to do with her at all. She would have felt anxious for a close friend, horrified, distraught. But strangely, for herself, she felt nothing. She listened to the doctor in genuine disbelief, as if he were talking about someone else, someone outside her world, a complete stranger.

When the consultation was over, he asked her if she had any questions. Sarah shook her head and smiled the smile she knew so well, the one she used for all occasions, the one that said: Don't worry, everything will be fine. It was a decoy, of course, a mask behind which her sorrows and questions and fears clustered. The truth was, she was a mess inside.

Sarah's smile was smooth, gracious, perfect. She didn't ask the doctor what her chances were, she refused to see her future summarized in a statistic. Some people wanted to know, but she didn't. She wouldn't let the figures seep into her consciousness, her imagination. If she let them, they would spread like the tumor itself, and undermine her morale, her confidence, her healing process.

In the taxi back to the office, she reviewed the situation. She was a warrior. She would fight. Sarah Cohen would handle this case like she handled all the others. She, who never (or hardly ever) lost in court, was not going to be scared by a mandarin, however malignant it might be. In the case of *Sarah Cohen v. M.* — because that would be the code name, she decided — there would be attacks and counterattacks and low cunning, too. Her enemy would not admit defeat easily, Sarah knew that: M. was vicious, the trickiest adversary she had ever faced. The trial would be lengthy, a war of nerves, a succession of hopes and doubts, and other moments when she would fear everything was lost. She must stay the course, give as good as she got. Wars like this were won over the long term, Sarah knew that.

Just as when preparing a case, she sketched the broad outline of her attack. She would say nothing to anyone. No one at work must find out. The news would be a bombshell to the team and, worse still, the clients. It would provoke needless anxiety. Sarah was a pillar of the practice, she was built into its foundations, she must stand strong, or the whole edifice would subside. And nor did she want their pity, their compassion. Yes, she was ill, but that was no reason for her life to change. She would be highly organized, no one would suspect a thing. She would invent a secret code in her diary, to cover her hospital appointments; she would justify her absences. She would need to be creative, methodical, sly. Like the heroine of a spy novel, Sarah would wage war underground. Like a secret extramarital affair, she would arrange to keep her illness out of sight. She knew how to do that, how to compartmentalize her life, she'd had years of practice. She would build the wall higher still, and higher again. She had kept her pregnancies hidden; she would do the same for her cancer. It would be her secret baby, her illegitimate child, its existence utterly unsuspected. Invisible, inadmissible.

Sarah returned to the office and got straight back to work. Imperceptibly, she watched for her colleagues' reactions, their looks, their tone of voice. No one had noticed a thing, she saw with relief.

No: she did not have the word "cancer" branded across her forehead; no one could see she was ill.

Inside, she was in pieces, but she would never let it show.

SMITA

Badlapur, Uttar Pradesh, India
Leave.

The thought had come to Smita like a command from heaven. They must leave Badlapur.

Lalita would not go back to school. The teacher had beaten her because she had refused to sweep the floor in front of her classmates. Later, the same children would be farmers, and her daughter would empty their latrines. There could be no question of that. Smita would not allow it. She remembers what Mahatma Gandhi said once, a doctor at the dispensary in the next village had told her about it one time: no one should have to clear away human excreta bare-handed.

It seemed that the Mahatma had declared the status of "untouchable" illegal, unconstitutional, a violation of human rights, but nothing had changed since. Most of the

95

Dalits accepted their lot without protest. Others converted to Buddhism to escape the caste system, like Babasaheb, the spiritual leader of the Dalits. Smita has heard of the huge ceremonies at which thousands of people change their religion. The movement was seen as a threat to authority, and anti-conversion laws had even been introduced. Candidates for conversion must obtain a permit or be prosecuted. A cruel irony: you might as well ask your jailer for permission to escape.

It was a choice Smita could not accept. She was too attached to the gods her parents had venerated before her. More than anything, she believed in the protection of Vishnu, to whom she had addressed all her prayers, morning and night, since childhood. She confided her dreams, her doubts, her hopes, to him. To abandon him would bring too much suffering. Vishnu's absence would leave a gaping void, impossible to fill. She would feel more orphaned even than at the deaths of her parents.

But she feels no attachment to the village where she grew up. The filth that she must clean relentlessly, day after day, has given her nothing. Nothing but the scrawny rats — the sad trophies that Nagarajan brings home at night.

They must leave, flee this place, it is the only way.

Smita wakes Nagarajan in the morning. He has slept deeply, while she has lain awake. She envies her husband's peaceful sleep. At night, he is a still lake, its surface untroubled, while she tosses and turns for hours. The darkness offers no respite from her torments. No, the dark only makes them echo, louder, more hideous than ever. In the dead of night, everything seems tragic, and final. Often, she prays that it will stop: the swirl of thoughts that leaves her no peace. Sometimes, she spends whole nights awake, her eyes wide open. People are not made equal when it comes to sleep, she thinks. People are not made equal at all.

Nagarajan grumbles as he wakes. Smita pulls him up from his bed. She has been thinking: they must leave. They can expect nothing from this life, the life that has robbed them of their dignity. It is not too late for Lalita; hers is just beginning. Everything is possible. Smita will not let the others take that from her.

My wife is raving, thinks Nagarajan. She has had another restless night. Smita insists: they must leave Badlapur. They say that in the city, there are places reserved for Dalits at school and university, places for people like them. They would have a chance there. Nagarajan shakes his head. The city is an illusion, a false dream. The Dalits are homeless there, huddled on the street or in the squatter camps that cluster all around, like warts on the soles of your feet. At least here, they have a roof over their heads and food to eat. Smita's anger flares: they eat rat meat, and they collect shit. In the city, they would find work, they would have dignity. She is ready to rise to the challenge, she has courage, she is tough, she'll take whatever is offered, anything rather than this life. She begs him. For herself, for him. For Lalita.

Nagarajan is wide awake now. Has she completely lost her head? Does she think she can take control of her own life just like that? He reminds her of the dreadful business that shook the village not long ago. The daughter of one of their neighbors, a Dalit like her, had decided to study in the city. The Jatts had caught her as she fled across the country. They had taken her to a remote field and raped her, eight of them, for two whole days. When she had returned home to her parents, she could barely walk. They had filed a complaint with the Panchayat, the village council, the lawmakers in rural areas. The council was controlled by the Jatts, of course. They left no seat for a woman, or a Dalit, though they were required to do so by law. Every decision taken by the council was binding, even if it was contrary to the Indian constitution. This parallel system of justice was never contested. The council had offered the family cash as compensation, in exchange for the withdrawal of their complaint. But the young woman had refused the tainted money. Her father had stood by her at first, but he had buckled under pressure from his community, and killed himself. He had left his family with no income and condemned his wife to the horrors of widowhood. She and her children were banished from the village. They were forced to abandon their home, and they had ended up destitute, living by the side of the road.

Smita knows this story. No need to remind her. She knows that here, in her own country, victims of rape are often considered culpable. There is little respect for women, still less if they are untouchable. These creatures that must not be touched, or even looked at, can still be raped, with impunity. Rape is meted out as punishment to the wife of a man who has got himself into debt. To the sisters of a man who commits adultery with a married woman. Rape is a powerful weapon, a weapon of mass destruction.

Some even talk of an epidemic. A recent judgment by a village council not far away had sparked widespread debate: two young women were sentenced to be undressed and raped in public to expiate the crime of their brother, who had run away with a married woman from a higher caste. The sentence had been carried out.

Nagarajan tries to reason with Smita: if they run away, they are sure to suffer terrible reprisals. People would come for Lalita, too. A child's life was worth no more than its mother's: both of them would be raped, and strung up from a tree, like the two young Dalit girls from a neighboring village last month. Smita has already heard the statistic; it makes her shiver: over two million women killed across the country every year, to the indifference of all. Victims of the barbarity of men. The whole world cares nothing. The world has abandoned them.

Who does she think she is, in the face of such violence, such overwhelming hatred? Does she think she can escape it? Does she think she is stronger than all the others?

But Nagarajan's terrifying arguments cannot break Smita's stubborn determination. They will leave by night, she tells him. She

100

will prepare their departure in secret. They will go to Varanasi, the holy city, sixty miles away, and from there they will take the train across India to Chennai: her mother's cousins live there, they will help them. Chennai is beside the sea; people say a man has created a fishing community for the scavengers, for people like her. There are schools for the Dalit children. Lalita will learn to read and write. They will find work. They will never have to eat rat meat again.

Nagarajan stares at Smita in disbelief. How will they pay for the journey? Train tickets cost more than everything they have. They have given their meager savings to the Brahmin, to send Lalita to school. There is nothing left. Smita lowers her voice. She is exhausted by her sleepless nights, but strangely, she feels stronger than ever, here in the dark hut. They will have to go and take their money back. She knows where to find it. She saw the Brahmin woman, once, hiding her savings in the kitchen when Smita went into their house to empty the latrines. She goes there every day. One minute is all it will take . . .

Nagarajan explodes: Is she possessed, by some *asura*?! Her dreadful scheme will get them all killed, her and all her family. He would prefer to eat rats all his life and catch rabies than go along with her crazy plans! If Smita was caught, they would all die, in the worst possible way. It was a dangerous game, and not worth the risk. There was no hope for them in Chennai, nor anywhere else. There was no hope for them in this life, only in the next. If they conducted themselves well, perhaps the cycle of re-incarnation would be kind.

Secretly, Nagarajan dreams of being re-incarnated as a rat, not the hairy, starving rats he catches with his bare hands in the fields, and grills over the fire each evening, but the sacred rats of the temple in Desh-noke, near the border with Pakistan, where his father took him once when he was a child. The temple's feral brown rats num-bered some twenty thousand. They are treated like gods, protected and fed by the local people, who bring them milk. The priest is responsible for their well-being; people bring them offerings from all over. Nagarajan remembers the story his father told him of the goddess Karminata: She had lost a child, and begged for it to be returned to her, but it had been reincarnated as a rat. The temple was built in homage to the lost son. Nagarajan's days out in the fields hunting rodents had taught him to respect them, he felt a strange solidarity with them, like a law enforcer who respects the outlaw he has been pursuing his whole life. Besides, he tells himself, the creatures are just like him: hungry and struggling to survive. Yes, it would be sweet indeed to be reincarnated as a rat in the temple at Deshnoke, and to spend your life drinking milk. Sometimes, after a hard day's work, the idea comforted him and helped him to sleep. A strange lullaby, indeed, but he didn't care, it was his.

Smita has no desire to wait for the next life. It's this life, here and now, that she wants, for herself and for Lalita. She reminds Nagarajan of the Dalit woman who has risen to the highest post in their state: Kumari Mayawati. An untouchable who has become a governor! They say she travels around by helicopter. She did not cower, she did not wait for death to deliver her from this life; she fought for herself and for all of them. Nagarajan becomes even angrier: Smita knows full well that nothing has changed, the woman who rose to prominence preaching the Dalits' cause wants nothing more to do with them now. She has abandoned them. She flies through the air while they flounder in shit. That's the truth! There is no one to lift them out of here, out of this life, this karma. Not Mayawati, not anyone else. Only death can free them. And while they wait, they will stay here in the village where they were born and have always lived. And with these words, delivered like the deadly swipes of a machete, Nagarajan leaves the hut.

So be it, says Smita to herself. If you do not want to come, I will leave without you.

GIULIA

Palermo, Sicily

Now every living thing
has voice and blood.
Now earth and sky
are a deepened spasm
racked by hope,
overthrown by morning,
flooded by your step,
your dawn breathing.*

Kamal and Giulia saw one another every
day. They had got into the habit of meeting
at the library at lunchtime. Often, they
would walk beside the sea. Giulia was
intrigued by this man, so unlike anyone she
had ever known. He didn't look or behave
like Sicilian men, and perhaps that was what
she liked about him. The men in her family

* Cesare Pavese, "You, Wind of March," trans.
Duncan Bush.

were authoritarian, outspoken, moody, set in their ways and attitudes. Kamal was the complete opposite.

She could never be sure he would come. Every lunchtime, when she walked into the reading room, she would look around for him. Sometimes he would be standing there, other times not. And this delicious uncertainty only served to heighten Giulia's curiosity. The butterflies in her stomach would wake her up at night — a new, exquisite sensation. She read and reread Pavese's poems. Their words were the only remedy for the lack of him that she felt now, so urgently.

It happened one lunchtime, when they were walking on the jetty. Giulia had taken him further than usual, to a beach unfrequented by tourists. She wanted to show him the place where she went sometimes to read — a sea cave that no one knew, she said. At least, that was what she liked to think.

The creek was deserted at that time of day. The cave was quiet, damp and dark, sheltered from the world. Giulia undressed without a word. Her summer dress slipped down to her feet. Kamal stood motionless, as if hesitating to pick a flower for fear of damaging it. Giulia held out her hand: the gesture was more than encouragement, it was an invitation. Slowly, he unwound his turban, removed the comb that held his hair captive. It unfurled like a skein of wool, down to his waist, black as jet. Giulia shivered. She had never seen a man with hair so long — only women. And yet there was nothing feminine about Kamal. He kissed her very softly, as one might kiss the feet of an idol, hardly daring to touch the surface.

Giulia had never felt anything like this; Kamal made love like an act of prayer, his eyes closed, as if his life depended on it. His hands were coarse from his nights at work but curiously, his body was soft, like an artist's brush on her skin. She trembled at his slightest touch.

After making love, they stayed wrapped in each other's arms for a long time. The women at the workshop would laugh about men who fell asleep right away afterward, but Kamal was not one of them. He held Giulia close against him, like a priceless treasure from which he could not bear to be parted. She could stay that way for hours, she thought, his body burning against hers, her pale skin against his, soft and dark.

They began to meet there, in the cave, beside the sea. Kamal worked nights at the cooperative, and Giulia worked days at the workshop. They met at midday. They made love at noon, and their embrace had the savor of stolen moments together. The whole of Sicily was hard at work, busy in the office, or the banks, or the markets, but not them. Those hours were theirs alone, they used and abused them, counting one another's freckles and marks, noting their scars, tasting every portion of each other's skin. Lovemaking by day is not the same as by night; there is something bolder, something strangely brutal, about discovering another's body in the full light of day.

Meeting one another in this way, it seemed to Giulia that they were like the tarantella dancers that she had watched as a child, at the street balls on summer nights: coming together, touching one another, moving apart — this was the dance of their relationship, governed by the ebb and flow of their work, their days, their nights. Frustrating, disconnected from life, but romantic in equal measure.

Kamal was a man of mystery. Giulia knew nothing about him, or very little. He never spoke of his past life, the life he had been forced to abandon to come here. Sometimes, watching the sea, he would gaze far into the distance; then, his cloak of sorrow would descend, enveloping him completely. For Giulia, water was life, a source of endless pleasure, sensuality itself. She loved to swim, to feel the water slipping over the surface of her body. One day, she had tried to lead him into the water. But Kamal had refused. *The sea is a cemetery,* he said. She had no idea what he had experienced, what the water had taken from him. He would tell her one day, perhaps. Or perhaps not.

When they were together, they never talked about the future, or the past. Giulia expected nothing of him, nothing but those stolen midday hours. All that mattered was the present, the moment when their bodies would come together as one, like two pieces of a puzzle, melding one into the other, a perfect fit.

Kamal never talked about himself, but he spoke readily about his country. Giulia could listen to him for hours on end. He was like an open book about a place that was deliciously unknown to her. She would close her eyes and feel as if she were stepping aboard a boat on which she was the only passenger. Kamal told her about the mountains of Kashmir, the banks of the river Jhelum, Lake Dhal, and its floating hotels. He told her about the red of the trees in autumn, the luxuriant gardens, the tulips spreading as far as the eye could see, to the Himalayas. Giulia urged him to tell her more; she wanted to know, she said. Tell me.

Kamal told her about his religion, his beliefs, the *Rehat Maryada,* the code of conduct that forbade Sikhs from cutting their hair or their beard, from drinking alcohol, eating meat, or gambling. He told her about his god, who preached a pure and whole life, a single, creator god who was neither Christian nor Hindu nor of any faith but who was ONE, that was all. Sikhs believed that all religions led to the same god, and that as such, all deserved respect. Giulia loved the idea of a faith without original sin, without heaven or hell. Heaven and hell existed only in this life, said Kamal, and it seemed to her that he was right.

The Sikh religion considers a woman to have the same soul as a man, he said. Sikhism treated both sexes alike. Women were allowed to recite hymns in the temple, to officiate at all the ceremonies, including baptisms. Women were to be respected, honored for their role in the family and society. A Sikh must treat another man's wife as a sister or a mother, and the daughter of another man as his own. As a symbol of that equality, Sikh names applied to both

110

sexes alike. Only their second name distinguished them. "Singh" for men, which meant "lion"; and "Kaur" for women — a word he translated as "princess."

Principessa.

Giulia loved it when Kamal called her that. She found it harder and harder to leave him and go back to work. How sweet it would be to spend whole days like this, she thought. Days, and nights, too. It seemed to her that she could spend the rest of her life making love to Kamal and listening to him talk.

And yet she knew that she had no right to be there. Kamal's skin, and his god, were not those of the Lanfredi. Giulia knew what her mother would say: a dark-skinned man, and not even a Christian! She would be mortified. The news would be all over the neighborhood. And so Giulia loved Kamal in secret. Their love was clandestine. With no official papers.

She returned to the workshop later and later after lunch. La Nonna was beginning to suspect something. She had seen the smile on Giulia's face, the new sparkle in her eyes. Giulia claimed to be going to the library every day, but she would come back out of breath, her cheeks aflame. One afternoon, La Nonna even thought she

111

could see sand in Giulia's hair, under her headscarf. The women began to gossip: Did she have a lover? Was he a boy from the neighborhood? Was he younger than her? Older? She denied anything was going on, and her insistence was tantamount to a confession.

Poor Gino, sighed Alda, his heart will be broken! At the workshop, everyone knew that Gino Battagliola, the owner of the neighborhood's hair salon, was mad about Giulia. He had been courting her for years. He came each week to sell his cut hair. Sometimes, he would come for no reason at all, just to say hello. All the women laughed about it. They laughed at the presents he brought her, to no avail. Giulia was unmoved, but Gino lived in hope, and came back time and again, tirelessly, bearing fig *buccellatini,* which the women all devoured.

In the evening, after the workshop had closed, Giulia would go to her father's bedside and read to him. At times, she felt guilty to be so alive in the midst of this tragedy. Her body was filled with joy, shimmering with pleasure such as she had never felt before, while her father was fighting for his life. And yet Giulia clung to her joy as a vital need; it was her way of telling herself that she would carry on, that she would not give in to pain and exhaustion. Kamal's skin was a balm, a salve, a remedy for the sorrows of this world. She wanted to be just that, a body abandoned to pleasure, the pleasure was what kept her on her feet, kept her alive. She felt torn between extremes, both defeated and exalted; like an acrobat on the high wire, she swayed with the wind. This is how it is, she told herself, our darkest and brightest moments come all at once. Life gives, and it takes away, all at the same time.

Today, Mamma had entrusted her with a mission — to go and fetch a paper from her father's desk at the workshop. The hospital was asking for some document, but her mother couldn't find it. *Dio mio,* everything is so complicated, she moaned. Giulia hadn't the heart to refuse. But she didn't want to go into Papà's office. She hadn't set foot there since the accident; she didn't want to touch her father's things. She wanted him to find the place just as he had left it, when he emerged from the coma. That way he would know that they had all been waiting for him.

She pushed the door of the old projection room, which her father had made his office. Slowly, she stepped inside. There was a framed photograph of Pietro on the wall, beside the pictures of his father and grandfather, three generations of Lanfredi, each one succeeding the other at the helm of the workshop. Farther along, other pictures were pinned up: Francesca as a baby, Giulia on the Vespa, Adela at her first communion, Mamma in her wedding dress, with her fixed smile. The Pope, too, not Francis but John Paul II, whom everyone admired the most.

The room was just as her father had left it before his accident. Giulia looked at his chair, his files, the glazed terracotta ashtray that she had made and given to him when she was little, in which he stubbed out his cigarette. His world seemed emptied of its substance, its life force, and yet strangely haunted. On the desk, the diary was open at the fateful page — July 13. Giulia could not turn it. It was as if her father was suddenly there, in the Moleskine diary with its black leather cover, as if a little of him lingered between the notebook's ruled lines, in the ink of its words, even in the small blot frozen in time at the bottom of the page. Giulia had the strange feeling he was there, in every molecule of air, every atom of furniture.

For a moment, she was tempted to turn around and shut the door behind her. But she didn't move. She had promised Mamma she would bring her the piece of paper. Slowly, she opened the first drawer, then the second. The third at the bottom was locked. Giulia was surprised. She felt a strange sense of foreboding. Papà had no secrets, the Lanfredi had nothing to hide. So why was the drawer locked?

Her mind spun with questions. Her imagination raced, like a horse released into the wild. Did her father have a mistress? A secret life? Had he been caught by the mafia? The Lanfredi had always kept out of it. Why these doubts, like a premonition, a dark cloud filling the horizon?

She searched, and quickly found the key inside a box of cigars, a present from Mamma. Giulia shivered. Should she even be here? She could still turn back . . .

With a trembling hand, she turned the key in the lock. The drawer opened at last. It contained a thick bundle of papers.

Giulia took them out.

And the ground opened beneath her feet.

SARAH

Montreal, Canada

Sarah's plan worked just fine, at first.

She took two weeks off for the operation. She needed three — the doctor had insisted, a week in the hospital and two weeks' complete rest at home, which she reduced to one without telling him. She couldn't honestly take more without arousing suspicion at the firm. She'd taken no vacations for two years, the children were in school — who would take three weeks in November, when hearings came thick and fast, like the snow that fell over the city?

She said nothing to anyone, not at work, not at home. She told the children she would be undergoing "a procedure"; "nothing serious," she added, so as not to worry them. She arranged for the twins to go to their father that week, and Hannah to hers — she had objected but gave in eventually. Sarah told them they wouldn't be able to visit her in the hospital — children weren't allowed, she said. A little white lie, she told herself, to ease the viselike grip on her heart. She wanted to spare them the horror of that place, the white hell with its bitter odor. The smells, more than anything else, were the reason she hated hospitals: the mixture of disinfectant and bleach that tied a knot in her stomach. She didn't want the children to see her there, like that: weak and vulnerable.

Hannah was especially sensitive. She trembled like a leaf in the tiniest breath of air. Sarah had noticed this about her daughter very early on — the impulse to empathy. She resonated with the suffering of the world, took it on board and made it her own. It was like a sixth sense, a gift. As a little girl, Hannah would cry whenever she saw another child hurt or scolded. She cried at news reports on TV, at cartoons. It worried Sarah at times: how would Hannah cope with that heightened sensitivity, being completely exposed to life's highs and lows, its joys and sufferings? Sarah wanted to tell her: protect yourself, arm yourself, it's a tough world, life is cruel, don't let yourself be touched or damaged, be like others, be selfish, insensitive, unmovable.

Be like me.

But she knew Hannah's sensitive soul. Sarah would have to accept that. And so no, she couldn't tell her. At twelve years old, Hannah would understand all too well what the word "cancer" meant. She would guess, above all, that the battle was far from won. Sarah couldn't burden her daughter with that — with the anxiety that went hand in hand with the disease.

Of course, she couldn't lie forever. Her children would ask questions eventually. She would have to talk, explain everything to them. The later the better, Sarah thought. She was taking a few steps back — ready to make the leap when the time came — but that didn't matter, it was her way of coping.

She didn't say anything to her father or her brother, either. Her mother had died of cancer twenty years ago. She wouldn't put them through that all over again, the emotional assault course, the roller-coaster ride: hope, despair, remission, relapse; she knew only too well what all those words meant. She would fight this alone, and in silence. She reckoned she was strong enough for that.

At the office, no one noticed a thing. Inès thought she seemed tired: You're pale, she said when Sarah returned from leave. Luckily, it was winter: bodies were hidden under

118

shirts, sweaters, coats. Careful not to wear anything low-cut, Sarah simply applied a little more makeup than usual and the illusion was complete. She perfected a code for her diary: "CA" for appointments with her consultant, and "lunch T" for her tests at the hospital, which she always booked between midday and 2:00 p.m. Her colleagues would think she was having an affair. And she rather liked the idea. Sometimes, she found herself fantasizing that she was meeting a man on her lunch breaks. A solitary man, in a town by the sea. A sweet, gentle affair. Inevitably, her daydreams stopped right there; reality dragged her back to the hospital, the treatment, the tests and examinations. Speculation was rife among the juniors at work: *She's out again today . . . and part of the afternoon yesterday . . . She switches off her cell phone, yes . . .* Did Sarah Cohen have a life outside the office? Who was she meeting over lunch, in the morning, and sometimes during the afternoon? Was he a colleague? A partner? Inès reckoned he was a married man, someone else suggested a woman. Why would Sarah take so many precautions otherwise? She came and went regardless. Her plan seemed to be working. For the moment, at least.

One tiny misstep would be her undoing,

as so often happens in crime novels; the devil was in the detail, lying in wait for the murderer. Inès's mother was ill. Sarah should have known. And thinking about it, she had been told, some time ago — last year. Sarah had said she was sorry, and then she had thought no more of it. The information was lost in the ether of her over-worked brain. Who could blame her? There was so much to think about. If she had taken the time to stop by the coffee machine, to roam the hallways, or sit down to lunch with her colleagues — which she never did — she might have heard it mentioned again. But the fact was, her exchanges with the others were limited to the bare, strictly professional, essentials. Not out of dislike or hostility, just a lack of time — she was never free. Sarah revealed nothing about her private life and didn't try to find out about other people's. Everyone was entitled to their own secret garden. In a different context, another life, she might have engaged more with her colleagues, even made friends. But in this life, there was no room for anything but work. Sarah was always courteous, but she was never familiar.

Inès was like her. She gave nothing away, never talked much about her life. It was a quality Sarah appreciated. In Inès, she could see the young lawyer she had once been. She had chosen her, when the firm was interviewing for the junior positions. Inès was hardworking, precise, and highly efficient. She was a brilliant lawyer, the best of her group. She would go far, Sarah had told her one day, *if she stacked the odds in her own favor.*

And so how could she possibly have known that Inès would be bringing her mother to the hospital that very day for a checkup?

Sarah had noted "CA" in her diary. Not the initials of her mystery lover, not Carl Asselin, the handsome lawyer on the neighboring team, with his uncanny resemblance to a young George Clooney. No, the "consultant's appointment" was with Dr. Haddad, Sarah's oncologist, who was not, alas, noted for his Hollywood looks.

When Inès had asked her, last week, for an exceptional day's leave, Sarah had agreed, made a mental note, and promptly forgotten. Things had a habit of slipping her mind lately, doubtless due to how extremely tired she was.

Soon, the two women would meet in a waiting room of the oncology ward at the university hospital. The same expression of surprise would register on both their faces.

Sarah would be rendered speechless. And Inès would cover the awkwardness of the situation by introducing her mother.

"This is Sarah Cohen, the partner I work with."

"Delighted to meet you, madame."

Sarah would be polite and give nothing away. It wouldn't take Inès long to figure out what her boss was doing there, in the middle of the afternoon, on a weekday, in a corridor of the oncology department, with a sheaf of X-rays under her arm. One moment from now, everything would come crashing down: the supposed affair, the lovers' lunches, the secret rendezvous, the late-afternoon trysts.

Sarah would be unmasked.

She tried to save face by claiming she had got the wrong waiting room, that she had come to visit a friend. She knew Inès wouldn't be fooled. Her colleague would quickly piece everything together: her two-week absence last month, which had surprised everyone, the string of out-of-office meetings that she had attended lately, her pallor, her weight loss, her collapse in court. Clues that now became proof, material evidence.

Sarah wanted to disappear, to dissolve, to soar into the air like the all-powerful superheroes the twins loved so much. Too late.

She felt suddenly stupid, trembling at the sight of a junior staff member, as if she had been caught red-handed, like a criminal. She didn't need to justify herself to Inès; she owed her nothing. Not her, nor anyone else.

Scrambling to break the uncomfortable silence that had settled over them all, Sarah greeted the young woman and her mother, then left with what she hoped was a confident stride. One question bothered her as she walked back to the waiting taxi: What would Inès do with the information? Would she divulge it? Sarah was tempted to go back, to catch up with Inès in the corridors and beg her to say nothing. But she stopped herself. To do so would be to admit her vulnerability and give Inès a measure of power, a lever.

She adopted a different strategy. Tomorrow, when she arrived at work, she would call Inès in and offer to make her second-in-command on the Bilgouvar case, the latest "hot" brief for the practice's most important client. Promotion — an unexpected offer to a young colleague who was sure to accept. Inès would be flattered; she would be in Sarah's debt. Better still, she would be dependent on her. One way of buying her silence, guaranteeing her loyalty. Inès was ambitious. She would understand that it was not in her interest to speak out and draw the ire of her senior partner.

Sarah left the hospital, reassured by the plan she had just devised. It was almost perfect.

She had forgotten just one thing: something her many years in the business had taught her. If you swim with sharks, best not to spill your own blood.

My work progresses slowly
Like a forest silently growing.
Mine is a demanding task,
A task that nothing should ever interrupt.

And yet I don't feel alone,
Shut up here in my workshop.

I leave my fingers to their strange ballet.
And reflect on lives I will never live
Journeys I never made
Faces I never saw.

I'm a link in the chain.
A humble link, but no matter,
It seems to me my life is here
In the three strands stretched out before
　　me,
In the hair dancing at the tips of my
　　fingers.

SMITA

Badlapur, Uttar Pradesh, India

Nagarajan has fallen asleep. Lying beside him, Smita holds her breath. His first hour of sleep is always restless; she knows she must wait if she is not to wake him up.

She is leaving tonight. She has decided. Or rather, life has decided for her. She never thought she would put her plan into action quite so quickly, but the chance has presented itself, like a gift from heaven. The Brahmin's wife has an abscess on her tooth and was forced to consult the village doctor that very morning. Smita was emptying their foul latrine when she saw the woman leaving the house. She had only a few seconds in which to act: such an opportunity would never come again. Cautiously, she had slipped into the storeroom near the kitchen and lifted the big jar containing their stock of rice, beneath which the couple kept their savings. It was not theft, she told herself, just the return of her rightful dues. She took back the exact amount they had paid to the Brahmin for Lalita's schooling, not a rupee more. The thought of stealing even one coin from another person, however rich, went against all her principles: Vishnu would show his anger. Smita was not a thief. She would rather die of hunger than steal so much as an egg.

She had slipped the money inside her sari and hurried home. Feverishly, she had gathered a few things, the strict minimum; she must not take too much. She and Lalita were both small and frail, they must not burden themselves. A few clothes and some rice for the journey, hurriedly prepared while Nagarajan was out in the fields. Smita knew he would not let them go. They have discussed her plan, and she knows where he stands. She has no choice but to wait until nightfall, praying that the Brahmin's wife will not notice anything before then. The moment she realizes the money is missing, Smita's life will be in danger.

She kneels before the small altar to Vishnu and begs for his protection. She asks him to watch over her and her daughter on their long journey, the nearly 1,500 miles they will cover on foot, by bus, by train, to Chennai. An exhausting, dangerous journey the outcome of which is unknown.

Smita feels a hot current pulsing in her veins, as if millions of Dalits were kneeling with her, praying with her, there before the small altar. She makes Vishnu a promise: if they manage to get away, if the Brahmin's wife fails to notice anything, if the Jatts don't catch them, if they reach Varanasi, if they manage to get aboard a train, and if they finally reach the South alive, then they will pay tribute to him, in the Tirupati Temple. Smita has heard talk of this legendary place in the hill town of Tirumala, less than 150 miles from Chennai: the biggest pilgrimage site in the world. Millions come there every year, it is said, to make offerings to Shri Venkateswara, the Lord of the Mountain, one of Vishnu's holiest forms. Her god, the protector god, will not abandon them, she is sure of that. She takes the small, dog-eared image before which she prays — a colored picture of the god with his four arms — and tucks it against her body, beneath her sari. Nothing can harm her if he is with them. Suddenly it is as if an invisible mantle has settled around her shoulders and enveloped her, protecting her from danger. Wrapped in its folds, Smita is invincible.

The village is swathed in darkness. Nagarajan's breathing is regular now. He is snoring gently through his nose. Not an aggressive rasp, more a soft purr, like a baby tiger nestled against its mother's belly. Smita feels a sharp pain in her heart. She has loved this man, become accustomed to his reassuring presence. She resents his lack of courage, the cloak of bitter resignation that he has thrown over their lives. She had so wanted to leave with him. She stopped loving him the moment he refused to fight. Love is fleeting, she tells herself, sometimes it leaves as quickly as it came, in the beat of a wing.

She pushes back the cover and feels suddenly dizzy. Is she mad to undertake this journey? If only she was not such a rebel, so unruly, if only the butterflies would stop fluttering in her stomach, then she could give up, accept her fate, like Nagarajan and their Dalit brethren. Go back to bed and await the dawn in a dreamless torpor, like an invalid waiting for death.

But she cannot go back. She has taken the money from under the Brahmin's rice jar; she cannot turn back time. She must throw herself body and soul into this journey that will take her far from here, or perhaps nowhere. She is not afraid of death, or even of suffering — she fears nothing for herself, or very little. But for Lalita, she is scared of everything. She reassures herself by repeating, over and over: my daughter is so strong. She knew it the day she was born. The child had bitten the village's birth attendant during her postnatal examination. He had laughed — the tiny, toothless mouth had left a minuscule mark on his hand. She's a tough character! he said. This six-year-old Dalit girl was barely taller than her schoolteacher's stool, and she had said no to the Brahmin. In the middle of the classroom, she had looked him in the eyes and she had told him, "No." Courage is not given solely to those who are well born. The thought gives Smita strength. No, she will not condemn Lalita to clear filth, she will not deliver her into that cursed dharma.

She bends over her daughter. The sleep of a child is a miraculous thing, she thinks. Lalita looks so peaceful, she feels guilty for rousing her. Her features are relaxed, regular, adorable. When she sleeps, she seems younger, almost still a baby. Smita wishes she didn't have to wake her in the dark and run away. The child knows nothing about her mother's plans; she does not know that tonight she has seen her father for the last time. Smita envies her innocence. She has long since lost that escape into sleep. Her nights offer nothing but a bottomless abyss, dreams as dark as the filth she cleans. Perhaps it will be different down there, in the South?

Lalita clutches her only doll tight against her, a present for her fifth birthday: a little "Bandit Queen," Phoolan Devi herself, with her red bandanna. Smita has often told her the story of the lower-caste woman, married at the age of eleven and famous for rebelling against her fate. As the leader of a band of *dacoits,* she defended oppressed peoples and attacked wealthy landowners who raped lower-caste girls on their land. She took from the rich to give to the poor and was a heroine of the people, considered by many to be an avatar of the war goddess Durga. Accused of forty-eight murders, she was arrested, imprisoned, then eventually freed and elected to parliament, before being assassinated by three masked men, in the middle of the street. Lalita loved her doll. All the little girls here loved Phoolan Devi. Her doll was sold at all the markets.

Lalita.
Wake up.
Come!

The child wakes from a dream known to no one but herself. She stares at her mother through sleep-filled eyes.

Don't make a sound.
Get dressed.
Quickly.

Smita helps her to get ready. Her daughter shows no resistance. She looks anxiously at her mother. What has come over her in the middle of the night?

It's a surprise, Smita whispers.

She hasn't the courage to tell her they're leaving and will never come back. It's a one-way ticket to a better life. Never again the hell of the village in Badlapur, Smita has promised herself that. Lalita won't understand; she will probably cry, make a fuss. Smita cannot risk ruining her scheme. And so she lies. A little white lie, she reassures herself, to sweeten the bitter reality.

Before leaving, she takes a last look at Nagarajan; her tiger is sleeping peacefully. Beside him, in her place, she has left a piece of paper. Not a letter — she has never learned how to write. Just the address of her cousins in Chennai, laboriously copied out. Perhaps their departure will give Nagarajan the courage he lacks today. Perhaps he will find the strength to join them down there.

Who knows.

With a last look around the hut, at the life she is leaving with no regrets — or so few — Smita takes her daughter's frozen hand and hurries out into the dark countryside.

GIULIA

Palermo, Sicily

Giulia had expected anything but this.

The contents of the drawer were spread out in front of her on Papà's desk: summonses from the bailiffs, final demands for payment, dozens of letters sent via recorded delivery. The truth struck her like a slap in the face. It could be summed up in a single word: bankruptcy. The workshop was crumbling under the weight of its debts. The House of Lanfredi was ruined.

Her father had said nothing. He had confided in no one. If she thought hard enough, she could remember one time, and one time only, when in the course of a conversation he had mentioned that the Sicilian tradition of *cascatura* was disappearing. Modern life, he had told her. Hardly any Sicilians kept their cut hair now, he had said. It was a fact. No one took care to keep anything anymore. People threw everything away and bought everything new. Giulia remembered their discussion around the table at a big family meal: soon, he had told her, their raw material would be in very short supply. In the sixties, the Lanfredi workshop had fifteen competitors in Palermo. They had all closed. He was proud to be the last. Giulia had known the workshop was experiencing difficulties, but she had never imagined bankruptcy was imminent. The possibility had never even occurred to her.

They must all face the truth. According to the accounts, the workshop could carry on for another month, at most. With no hair to treat, the women would be made redundant. The workshop was unable to pay them, the business would have to file for bankruptcy, and close.

Giulia felt crushed at the very thought. For decades, her whole family had lived on the income from the workshop. She thought of her mother, too old now to work, and Adela, in her last years of school. Her older sister, Francesca, had young children and did not go out to work; she had married a good-for-nothing who squandered all his wages on gambling — and Papà had often topped up their account at the end of the month. What would become of them? Papà had secured a loan against their family home: everything they owned would be seized. As for the workers, they would be unemployed. Theirs was a highly specialized trade; there was no other workshop like it in Sicily now that might hire the women. What would they do — that band of sisters, with whom she had shared so much?

She thought of Papà, down at the hospital, in a coma. Suddenly she froze. An appalling image sprang to mind: her father on his Vespa that morning, overwhelmed, distraught, riding fast, faster, and faster, on the steep roads . . . She drove the cursed thought from her mind. No. He could not have done such a thing, he would not have left them — his wife, his daughters, his employees — ruined, abandoned. Pietro Lanfredi had a highly developed sense of honor. He was not a man to flinch in the face of misfortune. And yet Giulia knew that his pride and joy, his success, the very essence of his existence, was the little workshop in Palermo that his father had run before him and that his grandfather had founded.

Could he have borne to see his staff laid off, his business liquidated, his life's work going up in smoke? She felt a cruel, gnawing doubt at that moment, like gangrene in a wounded limb.

A sinking ship, thought Giulia. And they were all on board: her, Mamma, her sisters, the women from the workshop. It was the *Costa Concordia.* The captain was gone and they all faced certain death by drowning. There were no lifeboats, no rings, nothing to cling on to.

The voices of her colleagues in the main workshop interrupted her thoughts. Like every morning, they were getting ready, talking about anything and nothing. For a second, Giulia envied their carefree mood — they had no idea what lay in store. She closed the drawer slowly, like an undertaker placing the lid on a coffin. She turned the key. She hadn't the heart to tell them today. Nor could she lie. She couldn't set to work alongside them as if nothing had happened. She sought refuge up there under the eaves, in the *laboratorio.* She sat facing the sea, just as her father had done. He could spend hours like that, gazing out at the horizon. He said it was a spectacle he never tired of. Giulia was alone now, and the sea cared nothing for her sadness.

At noon, she joined Kamal in the cave where they always met. She said nothing about her fears. She wanted to drown her sorrow in the texture of his skin. They made love, and for a moment, the world seemed less cruel. Kamal said nothing when he saw her cry. He kissed her, and their kisses tasted of salt water.

In the evening, Giulia returned home. She had a migraine, she said, and went upstairs to shut herself in her room and huddle under her sheets.

That night, her dreams were filled with strange images: her father's workshop broken up, their house emptied of its contents and sold, her mother drawn and distraught, the workers out on the street, the strands of hair scattered, flung into the sea, a whole stormy, tossing sea of hair . . . Giulia twisted and turned. She wanted to empty her mind and think of nothing, but the images kept coming, relentless, like an endlessly repeating dream she was powerless to escape, a sinister strain of music playing over and over again, stuck on a hellish loop. She was delivered from her torment, at last, when the dawn came. She rose and felt as if she hadn't slept, as if her head were clamped in a vise. Her feet were ice-cold; her ears buzzed.

She stumbled to the bathroom. A hot or cold shower would banish the nightmare, she hoped, and shock her exhausted body awake. She moved toward the bath and stopped.

There was a spider, right there in the bottom of the bath.

A small spider, with a slender body and graceful legs, like stitchwork on lace. It must have climbed up through the pipes and out into the white immensity of the enameled cast-iron bath, trapped there with no way out. At first, the spider would have struggled, tried to climb up the icy white walls, but its lacy legs would have slipped, sending it back down to the bottom. It knew now that it was pointless to struggle and stayed where it was, awaiting its fate, motionless, hoping for another way out. But which?

And then Giulia began to cry. Not at the sight of the black spider on the white enamel — though she had a fear of spiders and bugs; they provoked instant revulsion, uncontrolled panic. No, it was the certainty that, like the creature in the bath, she was caught in a trap from which there was no escape. And no one was coming to save her.

She was tempted to go back to bed and stay there forever. It would be so easy just to disappear. The prospect was enticing. She was at a loss to deal with so much sorrow, helpless against the great wave that had engulfed them all. One day, as a child, she had almost drowned on a family trip to the seaside at San Vito Lo Capo. The sea, usually so calm, had been rough. A wave bigger than all the others had knocked her off her feet, and for a few seconds she had felt cut off from the world, rolling in the surf. Her mouth had filled with sand; she remembered that to this day: a mixture of grit and tiny pebbles. For a moment she had no idea which way was up. Tumbling between earth and sky, the contours of the real world were obliterated. The powerful current had dragged her down, as surely as if she had been pulled under by her feet. In the semiconscious state that accompanies all accidents and falls, those moments when reality moves faster than thought, it seemed she would never reach the surface. That it was all over for her. She had almost resigned herself to the idea, when her father's hand had gripped her and pulled her back up to the surface. She had come to her senses, surprised, shocked. Alive.

But this tide will drag her down forever.

Fate held the Lanfredi in its grasp, thought Giulia. It was remorseless, like the earthquake that had struck at the heart of Italy again and again, always in the same place.

Her father's accident had left them badly shaken. But the death of the workshop would take them all down with it.

SARAH

Montreal, Canada

Sarah could sense it: something had
changed in the firm. Something very slight,
indefinable, almost imperceptible, but it was
there.

She noticed it first in a look, the pitch of a
voice in greeting, a certain over-keenness
when people asked how she was doing — or
didn't ask. And that tone of embarrassment,
that way of looking at her. The forced
smiles, or the avoidance of eye contact al-
together. None of it was natural.

At first, Sarah wondered what the matter
was with everybody. Was there something
wrong with her outfit? A detail she had
neglected? But, as always, she was impeccably turned out. She remembered, as a
child, how her schoolteacher had arrived
one day clutching a garbage bag. She had
placed it on her desk quite naturally, before
realizing that she had thrown her handbag

into the trash on her way out of the house that morning. She had got as far as school without noticing anything out of the ordinary. Of course, the children had burst out laughing.

But today, Sarah's appearance was perfect. She stared at herself for a long time in the bathroom mirror. Apart from her tired features, and her increasingly thin frame, which she had managed to hide, her illness had so far passed unnoticed. So why this hesitation, this new reserve in her dealings with colleagues? A curious sense of distance had established itself insidiously over the past few days, a distance that was not her doing.

It took just a few words from her secretary for Sarah to understand.

I'm so sorry, she said in a low voice, and her expression was sad and sympathetic. For a moment, just a moment, Sarah wondered what she was talking about. Had there been some disaster, a terror attack that she hadn't heard about yet? An unexpected storm, an accident, a death in the firm? It wasn't long before she realized that she herself was the bad news. Yes, she was the victim, the casualty, the one shrouded in grief.

Sarah stood openmouthed.

If her secretary knew, then everyone knew.

Inès had told them. She had broken their pact from one day to the next, without warning. She had revealed Sarah's secret. The news had blazed through the firm like a lit spark on a trail of gunpowder, down the hallways, into the offices, all around the conference rooms, the cafeteria, even up to the topmost floor, the pinnacle of the hierarchy, to Johnson himself.

Inès, whom Sarah had trusted. Inès, the valued assistant she had chosen and recruited herself. Inès, who smiled at her each morning, with whom she shared her caseload. Inès, whom she had taken under her wing. Inès, yes, Inès had stabbed her in the back in the cruelest way imaginable.

Tu quoque, fili mi.

Inès had confided their secret to the person most likely to divulge it: Gary Curst, the most jealous, the most ambitious, the most misogynistic of all the partners, the man who had nursed a visceral loathing of Sarah since her arrival. Inès, the traitor, would say she had acted in the best interests of the firm. I'm so sorry, she would say, though her contrite expression revealed otherwise. Sarah didn't believe for one second that Inès regretted what she had done. She should have known: Inès was subtle, she was *political* — that elegant expression which meant "knowing on which side your bread is buttered." Political meant "unafraid to use low cunning." Inès would go far. Yes, as Sarah had said once: *she stacked the odds in her own favor.*

Inès had been to see Curst, *thinking to act for the best;* she had told him that Sarah had made *mistakes* in the case they were handling — the Bilgouvar case, which was crucial for the firm's long-term financial health. Her *blunders* were perfectly *understandable,* of course, *given her condition.*

Sarah had never committed a single blunder. True, she had been finding it harder to concentrate since beginning her treatment, she was less focused, she forgot the odd detail, a name, or a term that had been used in conversation, but never in any way that had affected the quality of her work. She never missed a meeting with a client or colleagues. She felt weak and shrunken inside, but she tried harder still to make sure nothing showed. She had committed no *blunders* or *mistakes,* as Inès knew full well.

So why? Why betray her? Sarah understood too late, and the thought made her blood run cold. Inès wanted to take her place. She wanted to make partner. There were few chances of promotion in the firm.

Juniors were seldom bumped up the ranks. A weakened partner was a door left ajar, an opportunity not to be missed.

Curst was serving his own interests, too. He had always envied Sarah's close, trusting relationship with Johnson. She was clearly his next-in-line for managing partner. Unless something — or someone — blocked her rise . . . . He, Gary Curst, pictured himself in that seat, at the top of the pile. *A long illness,* as people said. A vicious, pernicious disease that attacked you, weakened you, a disease that could come and go, the ideal murder weapon, a fatal blow to an old enemy. Curst would come through it all spotless, with not a drop of blood on his hands. The perfect crime. Like a game of chess. A pawn falls; everyone moves one square forward. And the pawn was Sarah.

One word was all that was needed. One little word in a receptive ear, and the damage was done.

It was official now, everyone knew: Sarah Cohen was sick.

Sick — which meant vulnerable, fragile, likely to drop out in the middle of a case, to fail to see a piece of work through to the end, to take extended leave.

"Sick" meant unreliable, not to be counted

145

upon. Worse, someone who might leave forever in a month, or a year. *You never know.* Sarah heard the dreaded phrase, barely whispered, in the hallway one day: *you never know.*

Sick was worse than pregnant. At least you knew when a pregnancy would end. Cancer was sneaky; you might enter a period of remission, but then it might come back. It was there, like the sword of Damocles over your head, a black cloud that followed you wherever you went.

Sarah knew only too well that a good lawyer must be brilliant, effective, always on the offensive. A lawyer should reassure her client, persuade, seduce. In a big commercial firm like Johnson & Lockwood, there were millions of dollars at stake. She imagined the questions everyone would be asking. Could they count on her now, and for how much longer? Could they entrust her with the big accounts, the long-term cases that might stretch out for years? Would she even be there by the time they came to court? Would she be able to give up her time — the white nights, the weekends at work. Would she even have the strength?

Johnson called her into his office on the top floor. He seemed annoyed. He would have preferred the news to come from Sarah herself. They had always trusted one another — why hadn't she said anything? For the first time, Sarah realized that there was something in his voice that she disliked. That note of condescension, the pseudo-paternal tone he took with her — the tone he had always used, come to think of it. It made her sick. She wanted to tell him that it was her body, her health, she didn't have to keep him informed. That was the one thing she could still control: she could choose not to talk about it. She could tell him to fuck off, with his expression of false concern. She knew perfectly well what was worrying him: not how she was feeling, nor even whether she would still be there in a year's time, no, what really interested him was what she could still do; that was it, whether or not she could handle her case-load like before. In a word, whether she was still *worthwhile.*

But of course, she said nothing of the kind. She kept a cool head. With considerable aplomb, she tried to reassure Johnson: no, she wouldn't be taking extended leave. She wouldn't even take scraps of time off. She would be there. Ill, admittedly, but there. She would do her job and follow all her cases through.

Listening to herself speak, she felt suddenly as if she were standing before the judge and jury at a bizarre trial that had just got under way: her own. She was the accused, casting about for arguments to prop up her defense. But why? What was she guilty of? Had she done anything wrong? Why was she the one who had to justify herself?

Back in her office, she tried to tell herself that nothing would change. But she knew she was wrong. Deep down inside, she knew that Johnson was already looking around for alternatives.

Perhaps Curst — even M. — wasn't her worst enemy, after all.

SMITA

Uttar Pradesh, India

Smita runs through the sleeping country-side, with Lalita's tiny hand in hers. She has no time to talk, to explain to her daughter that she will remember this moment for the rest of her life as the moment when she made a choice, changed the course of their destinies. They run in silence, so as not to be seen or heard by the Jatts. When they wake up, Smita hopes that she and Lalita will be far away. There is not a second to lose.

Hurry!

They must reach the main road. Smita has hidden her bicycle there, in a bush beside the ditch, with a small bundle of provisions. She prays that no one has stolen it. They must travel several miles to reach National Highway 56, where they can get a bus, one of the famous green-and-white state buses that can be boarded for just a few rupees to

Varanasi. They are uncomfortable, and unsafe — at night, the drivers are often high on bhang — but the ticket price can't be beaten. It's less than sixty miles to the holy city. From there, they will find the station and board a train for Chennai.

Dawn breaks. The first rays of sunshine appear on the horizon. Already, on the main highway, the trucks are roaring by, and the din is terrifying. Lalita shakes like a leaf. Smita senses her fear: the little girl has never ventured far from the village. Across the road lies the unknown, the world, danger.

Smita pulls the branches away from her bicycle. It's still there. But the bundle of provisions lies torn apart in the ditch, a little farther away — a dog or hunger-stricken rats have eaten their fill. There is nothing, or almost nothing, left. They will have to continue on empty stomachs. There is no other choice; Smita has no time to find something to eat. Soon, the Brahmin's wife will lift the jar of rice before she sets off for the market. Will she suspect Smita right away? Will she raise the alarm with her husband? Will they hurry after her? Nagarajan will know they are gone, already. No, there is no time to find anything to eat, they must press on. The water bottle is intact, they have that at least for their breakfast.

Smita sits Lalita on the bag rack and climbs onto her bicycle. With her arms around her mother's hips, the little girl clings like a terrified gecko — the tiny green lizards that are so common in the houses here, and so beloved of children. Smita is determined that Lalita will not feel her mother's body shake. Tata trucks — of which there are a huge number on this narrow road — overtake them with a deafening racket. There are no rules here: the biggest, most powerful vehicle has priority. Smita trembles, gripping the handlebars — any fall would be catastrophic. She must pedal hard: a little farther, and they will join the NH56 that connects Lucknow to Varanasi.

Now they are sitting by the side of the road. Smita wipes a cloth over her daughter's face, and her own. They are covered in dust. They have been waiting for the bus for two hours. Will it come at all, today? The timetables are erratic, even hypothetical, here. When the vehicle comes into sight, at last, a dense crowd presses around its doors. The bus is already full. Getting on board is a tough business. Some prefer to climb up onto the roof and travel in the open air, clinging to the bars along the side. Smita clutches Lalita's hand and manages somehow to pull herself up inside. They find half a seat for them both, right at the back. It will do. Now Smita tries to fight her way back down the bus to fetch her bicycle, which she has left outside. It's a risky undertaking. Dozens of passengers cram the aisle. Some have nowhere to sit, some holler angrily at one another. A woman has brought chickens on board, sparking fury from a neighboring passenger. Lalita shouts, and points at the bicycle through the window: a man is riding it away, pedaling hard. Smita is pale-faced. If she chases after him, the bus will leave without her. The driver has just fired the ignition; the engine is roaring. Smita is forced to return to her seat, dead at heart. She watches the rickety frame that she bought a lifetime ago disappear. She had planned to sell it for food.

The bus shudders. Lalita presses her face to the rear window, eager to see everything along the way. Suddenly she springs to life.

Papa!

Smita is startled and turns to look: Nagarajan is there on the road. He runs toward the bus, which has just pulled out. Smita feels her strength desert her. Her husband is running after them, and the expression on his face is impossible to read: regret, confusion, love, rage? Very quickly, the bus outstrips him and accelerates away. Lalita begins to cry. She beats on the window, turns to her mother, begging her to help.

Mama, tell them to stop!

Smita knows that's impossible. She cannot fight her way down to the driver. And even if she could, he would either refuse to slow down and stop or force them to get off. She couldn't risk that. Nagarajan's silhouette shrinks into the distance; soon he will be a tiny dot far behind them. But still he runs, in vain. Lalita is sobbing. Her father is out of sight now. Perhaps forever. She buries her face in her mother's neck.

Don't cry.
He will join us in the South.

Smita wants to reassure her daughter, and convince herself of the possibility, too. But nothing is less certain. She wonders what else they will be forced to let go, before their journey's end. She consoles her weeping daughter and touches the image of Vishnu beneath her sari. All will be well, she tells Lalita. And there is comfort in her words. There will be challenges every step of the way, but Vishnu will be there, close beside them.

Lalita has fallen asleep. The tears have dried on her face, leaving faint white streaks.

Smita watches the landscape slipping by through the dirty window. Beside the road, makeshift shacks, a petrol station, a school, the wrecks of small trucks and vans, chairs beneath an ancient tree, a ramshackle market, traders sitting on the ground, a shop renting the latest motor scooters. A lake, warehouses, a ruined temple, billboards, women in saris carrying baskets on their heads, a tractor. All India is there, by the side of this road, she thinks. An indescribable chaos of ancient and modern, pure and impure, sacred and profane.

The bus arrives at the terminus in Varanasi three hours late — a truck had got stuck in mud on the road and blocked the traffic. Immediately, the cargo of men, women, children, suitcases, chickens, and everything the passengers had managed to cram overhead, underfoot, and between them on the seats spills out. There is even a goat, which a man fetches down from the roof while Lalita stares in amazement, wondering how he had managed to get the creature up there in the first place.

The moment they leave the bus, Smita and her daughter are caught up in the energy of the city. Everywhere, buses, cars, rickshaws, and trucks loaded with pilgrims converge on the Ganges and the Golden

Temple. Varanasi is one of the oldest cities in the world. People come here to purify themselves, to meditate, and marry, but also to cremate their departed loved ones, and sometimes to die. All along the ghats — the flights of steps leading down to Mother Ganges, "Gangaji" as the river is known here — life and death, dark and light, exist side by side in an endless dance.

Lalita has never seen anything like it. Smita has often told her about this city, a place of pilgrimage to which she had been brought several times as a child. Together, she and her parents had completed the Panchatirthi Yatra, an itinerary that involves bathing in five places along the sacred river, in a specific order. They had ended their trip with a visit to the Golden Temple, as custom dictated. Smita followed her parents and her brothers; she let them guide her. The journey had left a deep and lasting impression, an enduring memory — especially Manikarnika Ghat, one of several flights of riverfront steps reserved for the cremation of the dead. She remembers the burning pyre on which the body of an old woman could still be seen. In accordance with tradition, she had been washed in the Ganges, then dried, then burned. Smita had watched in horror as the flames licked at

155

the woman's body, then devoured her whole with a hellish crackling sound. Strangely, the dead woman's loved ones hadn't looked sad. Rather, they seemed to be rejoicing at their grandmother's *moksha,* her liberation. Some were chatting, others played cards, and some were even laughing. Dalits dressed in white worked at the site nonstop, day and night. Naturally, it fell to them to perform the cremations — that most impure of impure tasks. It was their job, too, to supply the tons of wood that were needed for the pyres. They brought the logs to the ghats by boat. Smita remembers the mountains of huge tree trunks waiting their turn on the quays lining the waterfront. A few feet away, cows were drinking the river water, indifferent to the scenes being played out along the banks. A little farther along, men, women, and children were making the ritual ablutions — traditionally, pilgrims immersed themselves in the Ganges from head to foot, for purification. Other groups — colorful and lively — were attending wedding ceremonies and celebrating with religious and secular chants. Some were washing their dishes, or even doing their laundry. In places, the water was black, its surface dotted with flowers, oil lamps — the pilgrims' offerings — and the decomposing bodies of animals, even human bones. After the cremations, the ashes were ritually scattered in the river, but many families could not afford a full cremation and tossed the departed's body into the water half-charred, or even whole.

No one is leading Smita today. There is no reassuring hand to cling to, only her daughter's. Lalita is following her now. They are alone in the anonymous throng of pilgrims, trying to find their way. The railway station is in the center of town, far from where the bus set them down.

In the streets, Lalita stares in wonder at the items displayed outside the storefronts, each more extraordinary than the last. A vacuum cleaner here, a lemon squeezer there, an entire bathroom, a washbasin, a toilet. Lalita has never seen one before. Smita sighs — she wants to move on, get farther, faster! But the child's curiosity slows them down. They come across a procession of schoolchildren in brown uniforms, all holding hands. Smita catches her daughter staring at them enviously.

At last, Varanasi Cantt Station appears, its concourse packed with a frenetic crowd. This is one of the busiest stations in the country. Inside the main hall, a tide of humanity presses toward the ticket offices.

Everywhere there are men, women, and children standing, sitting, or lying down to wait for hours, and sometimes days, at a time.

Smita tries to make her way through, avoiding the ticket touts who take advantage of the chaos and the innocence of tourists to extort a few rupees in exchange for dubious information and advice. Smita takes her place in one of the four ticket lines, each numbering at least a hundred people. They must be patient. Lalita is showing signs of fatigue — they have traveled all day on empty stomachs and have covered barely sixty miles. And the worst is yet to come, as Smita knows.

It is dark when she finally reaches the ticket office. The attendant looks surprised when she asks for tickets to Chennai that same day. The tickets must be booked several days in advance, he tells her. The trains are always full at the last minute. Hasn't she made a reservation? Smita's courage fails her as she contemplates spending the night here, in the holy city, where she knows no one. The Brahmin's coins are just enough for their third-class tickets and something to eat — a room for the night is impossible, even a dormitory. Smita insists. They must leave now, as soon as possible.

Without hesitation she adds almost all the coins she had set aside for their meal. The employee peers at her, hesitates, mutters something between his yellow teeth. He disappears and returns a few minutes later with two tickets for sleeper class, the cheapest there is, on the next day's train. The best he can do. Afterward, Smita learns that these tickets are sold to anyone who asks — there is no limit to the number of passengers in sleeper class. The railroad cars are permanently overcrowded. The employee has taken advantage of her credulity to relieve her of a few rupees. But by the time she understands what has happened, it is too late.

Smita carries an exhausted Lalita, who has fallen asleep in her arms. She pushes her way roughly through the crowd in search of somewhere to sit. All over the station, on every platform, people are getting ready to spend the night. They settle in, lie down, and fall asleep — if they are lucky. Smita sits on the ground in a corner, near a woman dressed in white, flanked by two young children. Lalita has woken up now. She is hungry. Smita takes out their water bottle. There is only a little left in the bottom, and nothing else for tonight. Lalita begins to cry.

Close by, the woman in white is giving her children crackers. She stares at Smita, and the little girl crying in her arms. She walks across and offers to share her meal. Smita looks up at her in surprise; she is unaccustomed to offers of help, she has never resorted to begging. Despite her low status, she has always kept her dignity. For herself, she would have refused, but Lalita is so frail, so thin, she will never make the journey if she does not eat. Smita takes the banana and crackers offered by the woman in white and thanks her. Lalita throws herself hungrily on the food. The woman has bought ginger tea from a passing tea seller and offers some to Smita, who gladly accepts. The scalding, peppery-sharp tea revives her. The woman — her name is Lakshmamma — engages her in conversation. She wants to know where Smita and Lalita are going. Don't they have a husband, a father, or a brother to travel with them? Smita replies that they are traveling to Chennai — her husband is waiting for them there, she lies. Lakshmamma and her two young sons are on their way to Vrindavan, a small town south of Delhi, known as the City of White Widows. She tells Smita that her husband died a few months ago, of flu. After his death, she was rejected by his family, with whom they lived. Bitterly, Lakshmamma tells her about the miserable fate of widows. They are cursed and held responsible for the deaths of their husbands, for having failed to keep their souls here on Earth. Sometimes they are even accused of using witchcraft to bring about their husband's sickness and death. They have no access to insurance if he suffers an accidental death and receive no pension if he is killed in combat. The very sight of them is considered an ill omen, even treading within their shadow brings bad luck. The widows are forbidden from attending weddings and festivals, forced to live in hiding, to wear white — the color of mourning — and to show penitence. Often, they are thrown out onto the street by their own families. Lakshmamma describes the cruel tradition of suttee, by which women in the past were forced to kill themselves on their husband's funeral pyre. Those who refused were outcast, beaten, or humiliated, and sometimes pushed forcibly into the flames by their in-laws, or their own children, to avoid having to share the inheritance with their surviving parent. Now, before being turned out onto the street, widows are forced to remove their jewelery and shave their heads, so that men will no longer be attracted to them. They are forbidden to remarry, whatever their age. In the country-side, where marriages are contracted at a very young age, some little girls find them-selves widowed at the age of five and are forced to beg for the rest of their lives.

"That's how it is: when your husband is gone, you have nothing."

Lakshmamma sighs. Smita knows this. A woman has no property of her own, every-thing belongs to her husband. When she marries, she gives him everything. And when she loses him, she ceases to exist. Lakshmamma has nothing, except a piece of jewelery she managed to hide inside her sari, which her parents had given her when she married. She remembers that magnifi-cent day, she tells Smita, when she was decked in fine jewelery and taken by her family to the temple for her wedding, amid wild celebrations. She had entered the estate of marriage in fine style and left it destitute. She would have preferred her husband to leave her, she says, to renounce her. At least then, she would not have been a pariah in the eyes of society. Her close family might even have shown her some compassion. But now, she met with nothing but scorn and hostility. She would have preferred to have been born as a cow — at least then she would have some respect. Smita doesn't dare tell her that she has chosen to leave her own husband, abandoning her village and all she knows. At that moment, listening to Lakshmamma, she wonders whether she has made a terrible mistake. The young widow admits that she thought about killing herself but had finally decided against the idea, fearing that her in-laws would then kill her two sons straightaway, to keep their inheritance — this happened sometimes. Instead, she had chosen exile in Vrindavan, with her sons. People say there are thousands of women seeking refuge there in charitable ashrams or "widow houses," or living on the streets. For a bowl of rice or soup, they will sing prayers to Krishna in the temples and earn enough to subsist. One meager meal per day — they are allowed nothing more.

Smita listens to the widow and says nothing. She is barely older than Smita herself. When she asks how old she is, Lakshmamma says she doesn't know, but she thinks she cannot be more than thirty. Her features are youthful, Smita tells herself. Her eyes are bright, but they express such infinite sorrow, the sadness of a thousand years.

It is time for Lakshmamma to board her

163

train. Smita thanks her for the meal and promises to pray to Vishnu for her and her sons. She watches as Lakshmamma walks away along the platform, holding her youngest son in her arms, and his brother by the hand, with no luggage but a flimsy bag knocking against her back. As she vanishes into the crowd of travelers, Smita touches the image of Vishnu beneath her sari and prays for him to accompany and protect Lakshmamma on her journey, and in her life of exile. She thinks of the millions of widows who share her condition, abandoned, destitute, and forgotten in a country that has scant regard for women, and suddenly she feels thankful that she is Smita, born a Dalit but whole, upright, and with the promise of a better life, perhaps.

I wish I had never been born, Lakshmamma told her, before she left.

GIULIA

Palermo, Sicily

When Giulia announced to her mother and sisters that the workshop was bankrupt, Francesca began to cry. Adela said nothing — she showed that typical adolescent indifference to the entire world, as if nothing could possibly affect her. Mamma sat in silence, then broke down. She who was ordinarily so pious, so devout, accused heaven itself of turning against them. First her husband, now their workshop . . . What crime had they committed, what sin, to deserve such punishment? What was to become of the children? Adela was in her last years of school. Francesca had made a bad marriage and struggled to provide for her little ones. As for Giulia, she knew nothing but the trade her father had taught her. The father who was no longer even there.

Mamma spent long hours crying that night, for her husband, her daughters, the

165

house that would be taken from them — she never cried for herself. With the first rays of the dawn, she had an idea: Gino Battagliola had been in love with Giulia for years. Everyone knew he longed to marry her. His family had money, hair salons across the country. Besides, his parents had always shown true friendship to the Lanfredi. Perhaps they would take on the loan Papà had secured against the family house? It wouldn't save the workshop, but at least they'd keep a roof over their heads. Her daughters would have somewhere to live. Yes, Mamma decided, Giulia's marriage would save them all.

She spoke to Giulia, but her daughter rejected the idea outright, and furiously. She would never be Gino Battagliola's wife, she would rather sleep out on the street! He was a pleasant enough man, she had nothing against him, but he was dull and bland. She often saw him at the workshop. With his lanky, awkward physique and that stubborn tuft of hair that refused to lie flat, he resembled one of the mildly ridiculous characters in Dino Risi's comedy *I mostri,* one of Papà's favorite films. He's a good boy, said her mother. Gino is kind, and he has money. Giulia would want for nothing, she was sure of that. Nothing except what really matters, Giulia reminded her. She refused to go along with the scheme, to lock herself in a gilded cage. She didn't want a life of convention and appearances. It was good enough for plenty, said her mother, and Giulia knew she was right.

Her mother's marriage had been a happy one, though in truth, she hadn't chosen the man of her dreams. Unmarried at thirty, she had finally agreed to the hand of Pietro Lanfredi, who had courted her assiduously. Love had come in time. Giulia's father had a fiery temper, but he was a good man who had earned his wife's affection. Perhaps it would be the same for her, too.

Giulia went upstairs and shut herself in her room. She could not accept her mother's choice. Kamal's burning-hot skin was all she wanted. She refused to slip between icy sheets, in a cold bed, like the heroine of *Mal di pietre,* the Sardinian novel that had made such an impression upon her: despairing of ever loving the man she had married, the heroine wandered the streets in search of her lost lover. Giulia did not want a life devoid of passion. She remembered La Nonna's words: Do whatever you want, *mia cara,* but on no account get married.

But what other solution was there? Could she face turning her mother and sisters out onto the street? Life was cruel, she thought, to lay the burden of her entire family upon her shoulders alone.

She couldn't face seeing Kamal, though she knew he would be waiting. Without really knowing why, she found herself walking to the little church her father had loved — and shivered as she realized she had begun to think of him in the past tense. She corrected herself. He was still alive.

She never prayed, but she felt the need to collect her thoughts. The chapel was deserted at this time of day. The quiet interior felt detached from the world; or perhaps the still, silent space lay at the heart of everything. Was it the cool air, the faint smell of incense, the ring of her footsteps on the stone floor? Giulia held her breath. Since childhood, she had always felt a sense of awe when she stepped into a church, as if she were stepping into a place of mystery, crowded with the souls of centuries past. There were always a few lighted candles. She wondered who found the time to tend the tiny, ephemeral flames amid the hustle and bustle of the world outside. She slipped a coin into the collection box, took a candle, and placed it in a holder next to the others. She lit it and closed her eyes. She began to pray, in a low voice. She begged heaven to save her father, to give her the strength to accept a life she had not chosen. The Lanfredis' redemption came at a heavy price, she thought to herself.

Only a miracle would get them out of this mess.

But there were no such things as miracles in this life. Giulia knew that. There were miracles in the Bible, and in the stories that she had read as a child. She had stopped believing in fairy tales. Her father's accident had propelled her into adult life, and she was completely unprepared. She longed to bask in the gentle warmth of late adolescence, like a delicious, long bath you don't want to end. But time raced on, maturity had come, and it was cruel indeed. The dream was over.

Marriage was the only solution. Giulia turned the question over and over in her mind. Gino would take over the loan secured against the house. The workshop was doomed, but her family would be safe, at least. As her mother said, it was what Papà would have wanted. And Giulia couldn't argue with that. Her mind was made up.

She wrote to Kamal that same evening. The words would be less cruel on paper, she thought. In her letter, she explained about the workshop, about the threat hanging over the family. She told him she would be getting married.

They had promised one another nothing, after all. She had never pictured a future with Kamal, never imagined their love would last. They didn't share the same culture, or the same god, or the same traditions. And yet their skin was a flawless match. Kamal's body fitted hers so perfectly. With him, Giulia felt more alive than at any other time in her life. She was disturbed by the violent desire that gripped her and kept her awake at night, that drove her trembling from her bed every morning. The feelings that took her back to him each day. This man she had only just met, and knew nothing about, or very little, had touched her more deeply than anyone before.

This isn't love, she thought, trying to persuade herself. It was something else. Something she had to let go.

She didn't even know where to send the letter. She had no idea where he lived. He told her once that he shared a room with another worker, somewhere on the outskirts of town. It didn't matter. Giulia would leave the letter in the cave where they always met. She would put it under a seashell next to the rock where they had embraced so many times.

Their story would end there, she told herself, as if by accident, the same way it had started.

She did not sleep that night. Sleep had deserted her the moment she discovered what lay in her father's desk drawer. She would watch as the hours passed, one by one. Sleepless, anxious nights, as if day would never break. She had lost even the strength to read, and lay still, like a stone, a prisoner of the dark.

She would have to announce the closure of the workshop to the women. She knew it was up to her; she couldn't count on her sisters, or her mother. The women who were more than her coworkers — her friends, she would have to send them away. There would be nothing to soften the blow, nothing to share except bitter tears. She knew what the workshop meant to each one of them. Some had spent their whole lives there. What would become of La Nonna? Who would hire her now? Alessia, Gina, Alda — they were all over fifty, a critical age on today's job market. What of Agnese, who was alone with her children now that her husband had left her?

And Federica, whose parents were no longer there to help her? Giulia had tried to put off the moment she dreaded, like a painful operation. But face it she must. Tomorrow I will talk to them, she told herself. And the thought of it destroyed her and kept her awake.

It happened at around two o'clock in the morning: a stone thrown up at her window in the dead of night. Giulia was startled out of the torpor into which she had finally sunk. A second strike rang out. She peered through the glass: Kamal was on the street down below. He lifted his eyes to hers. He held the letter in his hand and called out:

Giulia! Come down!
We need to talk!

Giulia signaled to him to keep quiet. She was afraid her mother would wake up, or the neighbors — they were all light sleepers. But Kamal stood his ground. He insisted. He had to talk to her. Giulia gave in. Hurriedly, she dressed, ran downstairs, and joined him in the street.

You're mad, she told him.
You're mad to come here.

And that was when the miracle occurred.

SARAH

Montreal, Canada

It started slowly, insidiously. First, a meeting at which someone had forgotten to include her. *We didn't want to bother you,* the partner told her later.

Then a case that no one had mentioned to her. *You've got enough on your plate at the moment.* Phrases calculated to show they cared. They were almost believable. Sarah didn't want special treatment, she wanted to carry on working, to be counted, like before. She wanted no one to make allowances. But she had sensed for some time that she was being involved less and less in the life of the firm, in the decisions to be taken, the management of the caseload. There were things people forgot to tell her, questions people would ask of someone else.

Since her illness had been made public, Curst had risen in the firm. Sarah saw him talking to Johnson far more often, laughing at his jokes, going out with him to lunch. Meanwhile, Inès was showing more initiative and taking greater liberties with the cases she handled, without consulting Sarah. When she called Inès to order, the junior would explain with a falsely apologetic air that Sarah *hadn't been there,* or had *been unavailable* — in other words, she had been at the hospital. Inès took advantage of Sarah's absences to make decisions and intervene at meetings in her place. She had become much closer to Curst lately and had even taken up smoking, solely — Sarah thought — in order to share cigarette breaks with her mentor. A chance of promotion . . . you never knew.

At the hospital, Sarah began her treatment. Ignoring the oncologist's advice, she refused to take days off work. If she was absent, if she abandoned her post, she left an empty space — it was too risky. She must hold on, every step of the way. She found the strength to get up every morning and make it in to work. She would not let the cancer rob her of the thing she had built up over so many years. She would fight tooth and nail to keep her empire. That thought alone kept her on her feet, gave her the strength, the guts, the energy she needed.

But the oncologist had warned her — the

treatment would be hard going, and the side effects even worse. He had given her an exhaustive list, in a spreadsheet, detailing the precise moment when she would feel nauseous, what would happen to her hair, her nails, her eyebrows, her skin, her hands, her feet. What lay in store, day after day, during the months of her treatment. Sarah had left his consulting room with a stack of prescriptions to counter everything on the list.

What he hadn't told her, what no one had mentioned, was the side effect that was more unpleasant than even the sore, swollen hands and feet, worse than the nausea or the fog that sometimes shrouded her brain. The side effect that she had been unprepared for, from which no prescription could offer relief: the isolation that went hand in hand with the disease itself, the slow, painful setting-aside that she was now experiencing.

At first, Sarah didn't want to put a name to what was happening at work. She preferred to ignore the things her colleagues had "forgotten," the new indifference in Johnson's eyes. Not indifference, exactly, that was the wrong word, but a kind of distance, a curious cooling of their relations.

It took several weeks of appointments to

which she had not been called, meetings to which she had not been invited, cases that had not been passed to her, before she was convinced: she was being pushed out.

The cruel, painful process had a name that she found it hard to contemplate: discrimination. A term she had heard in court a hundred times but which had never before applied to her. Yet she knew the definition of it by heart:

Discrimination may be described as a distinction, whether intentional or not but based on grounds relating to personal characteristics of the individual or group, which has the effect of imposing burdens, obligations, or disadvantages on such individual or group not imposed upon others . . .

The term applied to

behavior which would be considered discriminatory under the Human Rights Code, including humiliating, offending, or demeaning a person or group of persons on the basis of race, color, ancestry, place of origin, political belief, religion, family status, marital status, physical or mental disability, age, sex, sexual orientation, or conviction for a criminal offense unrelated to employment.

Discrimination was sometimes associated with the concept of stigma, as defined by the sociologist Erving Goffman: *The phenomenon whereby an individual with an attribute which is deeply discredited by his/her society is rejected as a result of the attribute.* The stigmatized person was set apart from those who perceived themselves as "normal."

Sarah knew it now: she was stigmatized. In a society that valued youth and vitality, she knew that the sick and the weak had no place. She had been a person of power and agency. Now she was tipping over into the opposite camp.

What could she do to counter it? She knew how to fight the illness; she had an armory of treatments and doctors at her side. But what remedy for exclusion? She was being gently pushed toward the exit, kept in solitary confinement. What could she do to reverse the process?

Yes, she would fight, but how? Take Johnson & Lockwood to court for discrimination? She would have to resign. If she left, she would have no help, no medical cover. How would she find another job? Who would take them on, her and her cancer? Could she set up her own firm? An attractive prospect, but she would need investors, and the banks would lend only to a person in good health, she knew that. And besides, which of the firm's clients would follow her? She could promise nothing, not even that she would be there in a year's time to defend their interests.

She remembered the dreadful business a few years ago — one of her colleagues at the firm had defended a woman who had worked as a medical secretary for a doctors' practice. She had complained of headaches, and spoken to the doctor, her employer, who had examined her. He made her undergo tests, then called her in to tell her she was fired: she had cancer. The official version was that she had been let go to cut costs, but no one was fooled. The case lasted three years, and the woman had won. She had died shortly afterward.

The discrimination being enacted against Sarah was less brutal. It did not speak its name. It was subtle, and by the same token, tricky to prove. But it was real nonetheless.

One morning in January, Johnson called her into his office, up on high. He asked how she was, with that fake air of concern. Sarah was fine, thank you. Having chemo, yes. He mentioned a distant cousin who had been treated for cancer twenty years ago and was doing just fine now. Sarah couldn't care less about all the stories of recovery people regaled her with now, at every opportunity, tossing them like bones for her to chew over. They changed nothing for her. She wanted to tell him that her mother had died of it, that she felt sick as a dog, that he could keep his false compassion, thank you very much. What did he know about ulcers all over your mouth, so that it was too painful to eat, feet that burned so that by the end of the day you could barely walk, about feeling so exhausted that the smallest staircase seemed impossible? His show of pity masked his complete indifference to the fact that in a few weeks' time she would have no hair, that her body looked so thin in the mirror it scared her, that she was scared of everything, scared of suffering, scared of dying, that she didn't sleep at night, threw up three times a day; that some mornings she wasn't even sure she could stay standing up. He could fuck right off with his caring concern. And his cousin could fuck off, too.

As always, Sarah was calm and polite.

Johnson got to the point: he wanted

another partner to join her on the Bilgouvar case.

Sarah couldn't believe what she was hearing. It took her a few moments to find her voice, to object. Bilgouvar had been her client for years, she didn't need anyone else to handle their interests. Johnson sighed and pointed to that meeting, the one meeting at which she had showed up late — she had got up at dawn to go to the hospital for tests before beginning her day at work. The scanner had jammed. Bad luck, said the technician apologetically, the last time that happened was three years ago. Hurrying to make up for lost time, Sarah had arrived at the meeting out of breath. It had barely begun. Of course, Johnson didn't care two hoots about that, he wasn't interested in Sarah's excuses, the hospital hardware, none of it mattered. Luckily, Inès had been there. She was always on time, he said. Just perfect. And there was the day Sarah had collapsed during a hearing that had to be postponed, he reminded her. He was speaking in a soothing, honeyed voice now — the tone she loathed more than anything — telling her that he-understood-she-had-her-treatment-plan and that everybody-here-wished-her-a-full-and-speedy-recovery. Johnson was great at that, the ready-made phrases that sounded false, and hollow, and didn't mean a thing. Sarah was-in-need-of-support, that was the-true-spirit-of-this-firm, we-understand-the-true-meaning-of-teamwork.

To support-her-through-this-difficult-time she would be working-from-now-on with . . . Gary Curst.

If Sarah hadn't been sitting down, she would have dropped to the floor.

She would have preferred anything, anything at all, to that.

She would rather be fired. She would rather be slapped and insulted — at least then she would know where she stood. Anything but this slow, unbearable death by isolation. She felt like a bull being sacrificed in the ring. She knew it was pointless to object, nothing she could say would change his mind. Her fate was sealed. Johnson had made his decision. She was sick, and no longer of any use. No one could count on her now.

Gary Curst would swallow the Bilgouvar case whole. He would take her biggest client. Johnson knew how he operated. Together, they were picking her apart, while she was still alive. Sarah wanted to shout for help, to cry "Stop thief!" like a character in a kids' cartoon. But it was a cry in the wilderness. There was no one to hear her, no one to come to her aid. The thieves were impeccably dressed, the ambush was invisible, even respectable and well-intentioned. A smart attack, perfumed with expensive cologne — aggression in a three-piece suit.

Gary Curst was exacting his revenge. With the Bilgouvar case in his portfolio, he would become the most powerful partner in the firm, the dream successor to Johnson. He wasn't ill or weak; in fact, he was at the height of his powers, like a vampire engorged with the blood of others. At the end of the interview, Johnson gazed at Sarah with sad eyes and uttered the cruelest of phrases: *You look tired, you should go home and get some rest.*

Sarah returned to her office, destroyed. She had expected to be dealt some blows, but she hadn't expected this. When the news broke a few days later, she wasn't even surprised: Curst had been appointed managing partner. He would succeed Johnson in the top job, at the head of the firm. The appointment sounded the death knell for Sarah's career.

That day, she went home in the middle of the afternoon. This was something new to her — an hour alone in her empty house. Silence reigned. She sat on her bed and began to cry, because she was thinking about the woman she had been, even yesterday: a strong, determined woman with a place in the world — and it seemed to her that today, the world had abandoned her to her fate.

There was nothing to break her fall now. The long descent had only just begun.

This morning, one of the strands broke.
It seldom happens.
But it happened today.

It's a disaster, a tidal wave
On a microscopic scale,
That wrecks the work of several days.

I think of Penelope on Ithaca, then,
Tirelessly reworking
Each day what she destroys in the night.

I must start all over again.
It will be a beautiful piece,
The thought consoles me.
Never lose the thread.
I must hold on.
Start over and go on.

SMITA

Varanasi, Uttar Pradesh, India

Smita wakes with a start on the station platform where she had dozed off, with Lalita curled tight against her. In the first light of dawn, hundreds of people are running, carrying everything with them, in the direction of a train that has just pulled in. Frantically, Smita wakes her small daughter.

Come!
The train is here!
Quickly!

Hurriedly, she gathers their things — she has slept on their bag to protect it from thieves — then clutches her daughter's hand and hurries toward the third-class railcar. The crowd throngs the platform, a great wave of people, pushing and elbowing and trampling on one another's feet.

Shouts of *Chalo, chalo!* ring out everywhere.

Come on, come on!

Smita grabs the handle of the railcar door. The crowd presses hard all around them; she clings on tight. She tries to get Lalita on board before her, afraid the little girl will suffocate in the crush of desperate passengers. Suddenly she is seized with doubt and turns to the gaunt man beside her. Is this the train to Chennai? she shouts over the din. No! he replies, this one's going to Jaipur, you shouldn't trust the signs, they are often wrong.

Smita pulls Lalita back and fights her way through the crowd, like a salmon swimming upriver.

After several journeys back and forth across the station, a wealth of contradictory information and one — vain — attempt to ask a station official, Smita and Lalita find the train to Chennai, at last. They climb into the blue sleeper-class railcar. The dilapidated interior has no air-conditioning; cockroaches scuttle on the floor. Mother and daughter squirm their way into the packed railcar and find a tiny space on a bench seat. Twenty people have already piled into the space that measures barely a few square feet. Overhead, more men and women occupy the narrow upper bunks. Their legs dangle in midair. It will be a long journey: over 1,200 miles, crammed in like this. Theirs is a local service, cheaper than the express. It trundles along slowly and stops everywhere. A journey across India — what madness, thinks Smita. The whole of humanity is on the move, piled one on top of the other, suffocating, exhausted, in these third-class railcars. Everywhere there are families, babies, old people sitting on the floor or standing, packed so tight they can barely move.

The first hours of the journey pass without difficulty. Lalita is asleep; Smita dozes in a half-conscious, dreamlike state. Suddenly the little girl wakes, desperate to use the toilet. Smita tries to make her way through with her daughter to the end of the railcar. It's a dangerous business, difficult not to trample the many passengers sitting on the floor. She takes care but treads on someone by accident and earns a furious, shouted tirade.

They reach the toilet door, to find it double locked. Smita tries to open it, bangs on it repeatedly with her fist. There is no point in trying, says an elderly, toothless woman with leathery, parchment-dry skin sitting on the floor nearby. They've been shut in there for hours. A whole family, looking for somewhere they could sleep and sit down. They won't open up until the end of the line, everyone tells Smita. She hammers on the door, ordering then begging the family to come out. No point in shouting, says the old lady, others have tried before you. There is nothing to be done. My daughter really needs to go, whispers Smita. The old, toothless lady points to a corner of the railcar: just tell her to go there. Or wait for the next stop. Lalita looks paralyzed; she does not want to relieve herself in front of all the other passengers; she is only six years old, but already she has an acute sense of personal dignity. Smita makes it clear that she has no choice. They cannot risk getting off at the next stop, there will be too little time. At the previous station, one family was caught out — the platform was packed with people and they had been unable to get back on board the train. It had left without them, abandoning them in the middle of nowhere, in an unfamiliar station with no luggage and no money.

Lalita shakes her head. She would rather wait. There will be a longer stop in an hour or two, in Jabalpur. She will hold on until then.

A foul smell fills the railcar as they make their way back to their bench. The mixed stench of urine and excrement. It is the same at every stop. For many of the townspeople, the edges of the railway lines are their toilet. Smita knows that smell all too well: it's the same anywhere, it knows no frontier, it ignores rank, caste, and wealth. She is used to it, but she holds her breath nonetheless, just as she did when making her rounds. She places a scarf over her nose, and does the same for Lalita. Never again. This is her promise to herself. Never again to have to hold her breath. To breathe freely, with dignity, at last.

The train pulls away. The vile smell subsides, leaving the suffocating but less nauseating reek of cramped, sweaty bodies. Soon it will be midday. The heat is unbearable in the packed compartments, with a single fan to stir the fetid air. Smita makes Lalita take some water and gulps a few mouthfuls herself.

The journey stretches out, dank and torpid. Some people are polishing their shoes. Others gaze out at the landscape through the half-open door or press against the barred windows, hoping for some fresh air, when all that pours in is the hot breath of the tropics. A man makes his way through

189

the train reciting prayers and sprinkling water over the travelers' heads, as a sign of blessing. A beggar sweeps the railcar floor and asks for a few rupees for its upkeep. He tells his miserable tale to anyone who will listen. He was working in the fields with his family in the north when the rich farmers came looking for his father, who owed them money. They had beaten him, broken his limbs, and torn out his eyes, then dragged him away by the feet, in front of his entire family. Lalita shudders at the horrific story. Smita scolds the beggar: he should go and sweep and tell his story somewhere else, there are children here.

Beside her, a plump woman soaked in sweat talks about her journey to the temple in Tirupati to make an offering. Smita is roused from her torpor. The woman's son had fallen ill, the doctors said there was no hope. A healer had advised her to make a temple sacrifice, and her son had been healed! Today, she was on her way to give thanks to Vishnu for the miracle by placing food and wreaths of flowers at the foot of his statue. To do so, she has undertaken a journey of several thousand miles. She complains about the conditions of travel, but that's how it is, she says, adding: the god himself decides whether the path that leads to him is hard or painless.

Night falls. In the railcar, people organize themselves to try to get some semblance of rest. The bench seats fold out into couchettes, but sleep is difficult nonetheless. Smita dozes off at last, hugging Lalita's tiny body tight, beside the voluptuous woman. She thinks again about the promise she made to Vishnu before beginning her journey. She must keep her word.

And so she makes a decision, there on the couchette, in the black of night, somewhere between the states of Chhattisgarh and Andhra Pradesh: tomorrow, she and Lalita will not continue their journey to Chennai, as she had planned. When the train stops at the station in Tirupati, they will get down and climb the holy mountain to pay homage to their god. With that thought, Smita feels suddenly at peace and falls deeply asleep.

Yes, Vishnu is waiting for them.

Her god is here, at their side.

GIULIA

Palermo, Sicily

Giulia joined Kamal in the street, outside her house. She stood facing him and felt suddenly feverish. What was he going to say? That he loved her? That he didn't want her to leave? Perhaps he was going to try to stop her, to prevent the senseless marriage. Giulia imagined a passionate embrace, long and sad goodbyes, like characters in the soaps Mamma watched all day long. But part they must.

Kamal was not in the least bit tearful. Rather, he seemed excited, impatient. There was a curious light in his eyes. He spoke in a low voice, quickly, as if confiding a secret.

I might have a solution, he told her, *for the workshop.*

Without another word of explanation, he took her by the hand and led her to the sea, to their cave. Giulia could barely make out his features in the darkness. He had read her letter: the workshop didn't have to close, he told her. He had a solution that could save them. She stared at him in disbelief — what was this strange energy that gripped him? Kamal was usually so calm, but now he seemed exultant, inspired. He carried on talking: the Sikhs' code of conduct forbade them from cutting their hair, but there was no such rule for the Hindus in his country. Thousands of them cut their hair in the temples, he explained, as an offering to the gods. The act of shaving one's head was sacred, but the hair itself was not: it was collected and sold on the open market. Some people had even built businesses around the practice. If the raw material for the workshop was in short supply here, he concluded, they must fetch it from India.

Import. It was the only way to save the workshop.

Giulia was at a loss for words. She felt amazement and disbelief all at once. Kamal's idea seemed absurd. Indian hair. What a strange idea. Of course, she knew how to treat it. She knew her father's chemical formula, how to discolor the hair until it turned milky white, ready to be dyed. She knew the formula, and the process. But the idea scared her. There was something barbaric about the idea of "importing"; the word had a foreign ring to it. It was not the language of here, of the little workshops. The hair that was treated and re-dyed by the Lanfredi came from Sicily, and always had. It was local hair, island hair.

When a source runs dry, another must be found, said Kamal. If Italians were no longer selling their hair, the Indians were giving it away! People visited the temples in their thousands, every year. The hair was sold by the ton. A rich, virtually inexhaustible supply.

Giulia didn't know what to think. The idea seemed appealing one minute and totally beyond her grasp the next. Kamal was sure he could help her. He spoke the language, he knew the country. He could be the link between India and Italy. What a wonderful man this is, she thought. Anything seems possible to him. She felt cross at her own despair and skepticism.

She walked home with her thoughts on fire. Her mind was jumping like a monkey in a cage. She found it impossible to calm down. She couldn't sleep, it was pointless to try. She turned on her computer and spent the rest of the night searching feverishly.

What Kamal had said was true. Online, she found pictures of Indian men and women in the temples. In hopes of a good harvest, a happy marriage, or better health, men and women would offer their hair to the gods. Mostly, they were "untouchable," the poorest in society. Their hair was all they had to give.

She read an article about an English businessman who had made a fortune importing hair. Now he was well-known all over the world and traveled in a private helicopter. Strands of Indian hair were delivered by the ton to his factory near Rome. The merchandise was flown to the airport at Fiumicino, then taken to an industrial estate on the north side of the city, where it was treated in vast workshops. Indian hair was the best in the world, declared the businessman. Reclining poolside at his villa near Rome, he explained how the hair was disinfected and disentangled, plunged into vats to be discolored, then dyed blond, chestnut, red, or auburn, made to resemble European hair exactly. *We turn the black gold to blond,* he said, with some satisfaction. Then the strands were sorted by length, collected into packets, and dispatched all around the world, to be made into extensions or wigs. Fifty-three countries, twenty-five thousand hair salons — the figures were dizzying! His company had become a multinational. People had joked about his strange idea at first, he said. But the business had prospered. Today, he employed five hundred people at production sites on three continents, he concluded proudly: 80 percent of the global market for hair.

Giulia was doubtful. Everything seemed so simple to the English businessman. Could she do the same? How could she accomplish anything of the kind? Who did she think she was? Turning a family business into an industrial enterprise was a hopeless dream. And yet the Englishman had done it. And if he had succeeded, why not her?

One question bothered her more than anything else: What would her father say? Would he support her plan? He always said you should think big, be bold and enterprising. But he was fiercely devoted to his island roots, his identity. Sicilian hair! he would say proudly, pointing to the strands. Would change mean betrayal?

Giulia thought of his photograph in the office, beside those of his father and grandfather. Three generations of Lanfredi, succeeding one another at the head of the workshop. And she decided that to give up now would be treachery indeed. The destruction of everything they had worked for, all their lives: Wouldn't that be the ultimate betrayal?

Suddenly she wanted more than anything to believe in Kamal's plan. The workshop would not go under. She would not marry Gino Battagliola. Kamal's idea was a gift from heaven, a piece of luck, an act of providence. It's the *Costa Concordia,* she had thought, staring at the contents of her father's desk drawer, but it seemed to her now that a ship was advancing through the darkness to save them and throw them a life preserver.

Suddenly she understood that she had not met this man by chance, on the Feast of Santa Rosalia. He had been sent to her. Heaven had heard her prayers and answered them.

There it was, the miracle she had been waiting for.

SMITA

Tirupati, Andhra Pradesh, India
Tirupati! Tirupati!

A man in the railcar is calling out the next stop. Soon, the train will reach the station in Tirupati. The brakes screech on the rails. Immediately, pilgrims pour out onto the platform, laden with blankets, luggage, tin pots, provisions, flowers, offerings, children in their arms, old people on their backs. Everyone presses toward the exit leading to the sacred mountain. Caught in the tide, unable to resist the flow, Smita clutches Lalita's hand. Terrified that her daughter might be swept away, she takes her in her arms. The station seethes like an anthill. There are tens of thousands of people here. People say the sanctuary receives fifty thousand pilgrims every day, and ten times that on feast days. Everyone comes to honor Venkateswara, Lord of the Seven Hills, one of the forms of Vishnu. It is said he has the

198

power to grant any request that is made in his presence. His huge statue lies within the temple sanctuary of Tirumala, at the top of the sacred hill, overlooking the town that spreads out at its foot.

Surrounded by thousands of ardent worshippers, Smita feels a kind of exaltation mingled with terror. She feels tiny, an insignificant speck in this crowd, like nothing she has ever experienced before. And at the same time, she shares their excitement. Everyone has come here in the hope of a better life, or to give thanks for some favor, a piece of good fortune: the birth of a son, the healing of a loved one, a happy marriage.

To reach the temple, some cram into the buses that, for a fare of forty-four rupees, take pilgrims to the top of the hill. But everyone knows that a true pilgrim climbs the hill on foot. Smita has not come this far to take the easy path now. She removes her sandals, and Lalita's, too, in accordance with tradition. Many are doing the same, removing their shoes as a sign of humility before climbing the steps that lead to the sanctuary gates.

Three thousand six hundred steps, about ten miles, three hours of effort! says a fruit seller sitting on the side of the path. Smita is worried about Lalita. The little girl is tired; they have barely slept on the uncomfortable, overcrowded train. But there is no turning back now. They will go at their own pace, if it takes them all day. Vishnu is watching over them, he has brought them here, they cannot fail him, now that they are so close. Smita spends a few rupees on some coconut, which Lalita devours hungrily. She keeps a whole nut to break on the first step as an offering to the god — as is the custom. Some light small candles, which they place on each step, others anoint the steps with bright ocher and purple pigment mixed with water. The most pious, determined pilgrims climb on their knees. Smita sees an entire family advancing slowly in this way, wincing with pain at each step climbed. Such self-denial, she thinks. She envies and admires them.

A quarter of the way up, Lalita is showing signs of fatigue. They stop to drink and catch their breath. After an hour of walking, the little girl can take no more. Smita hoists her daughter's tiny body onto her back for the rest of the climb. She is small and thin herself, and close to exhaustion, but she is determined to achieve her aim. She focuses her mind on the image of the beloved god, before whom she will soon be standing.

Vishnu has given her extraordinary strength today, it seems, in order that she, Smita, might get to the top and prostrate herself before him.

Lalita has been sleeping for a while when Smita completes her climb. She sits down in front of the temple gates, breathing hard. The holy space is enclosed by high walls. A gigantic white tower, in the Dravidian style, rises up into the sky. Smita has never seen anything like it. Tirumala is a world all of its own, more densely populated than a city. In accordance with tradition, no alcohol, meat, or cigarettes are sold here. Admission to the temple complex is by ticket — the cheapest is twelve rupees, an elderly pilgrim tells Smita. A crowd of people press forward to the ticket booths, at which a face appears from time to time. Smita understands now that the arduous climb was just a taster of what lies ahead. They will have to wait for hours before they can hope to enter the sanctuary.

It is late, night is falling. Smita needs to rest. She must sleep a little, at least try. A man approaches through the crowd of flower and souvenir sellers around the temple gates. He has seen her looking lost and utterly exhausted. There are free dormitories for the pilgrims, he tells her. He can show her the way. He peers into her face, and his gaze lingers over Lalita. He can take them there, in exchange for one or two favors. Smita grips her daughter's hand and pulls her sharply away from the predator. And yet he had such a kind, friendly look, like an angel . . . She shudders at the thought of a night sleeping rough. Two females traveling alone are easy prey. They must find shelter, it is a matter of survival. A sadhu sitting at the side of the road, dressed in a yellow *longhi* — the Vishnuites' color — points out which way she should go.

The first dormitory is closed, the second is full. At the entrance to the third, an elderly woman announces that she has just one bed left. That doesn't matter. Smita and Lalita have shared so much that they feel they are one and the same. They enter a run-down hall furnished with rows of simple beds placed one against the other. And despite the loud murmur filling the room, they sink into a deep sleep.

SARAH

Montreal, Canada

Sarah had taken to her bed and stayed there for three days.

Yesterday, she had called the doctor and asked him to sign her off work — for the first time in her career. She did not want to go back to the office. She couldn't stand the hypocrisy, the unfair sidelining to which she had been subjected.

First came denial, then incredulity. Then anger, an uncontrolled rage that possessed her utterly. And after the rage, defeat, like a vast, immeasurable expanse of desert offering no escape.

Sarah had always been the master of her own choices, her direction in life; she was the archetypal executive: *"A person having administrative or supervisory authority in an organization, who makes decisions and puts them into action."* But now, she was being subjected to other people's decisions. She felt betrayed, disowned, like a woman scorned, one who has fallen short of expectations and been judged inept, inadequate, useless.

She had broken through the glass ceiling, only to hit the invisible wall that separated the healthy and the sick. She was in the second camp now, weak and vulnerable. Johnson and his fellow partners were burying her alive. They had tossed her body into a ditch, and now they were covering her slowly with shovel after shovel of smiles and false sympathy. Professionally, she was dead. She knew it. As if in a nightmare, she was the helpless spectator of her own burial. She could shout and scream that she was there, alive and kicking inside the coffin, but no one was listening. Her torment felt like a hideous waking dream.

Every last one of them was lying. They told her to "be strong," that she "would get through this," but their actions said the exact opposite. They had dropped her. Like a broken piece of furniture left out for collection. She was blacklisted.

She had sacrificed everything for her work, and now *she* was the sacrificial victim, on the altar of cost-efficiency and performance. Here, it was sink or swim. She could go right ahead and drown now.

Her plan had failed. Her wall had collapsed, undermined by Inès's naked ambition. She had been overtaken on the inside by Curst, with Johnson's blessing. She had thought he at least might have been on her side, or have tried to help her, but he had deserted her without a second thought. He had taken from her the one thing that had kept her on her feet, the one thing that had given her the strength to get up each morning: her place in society, her professional life, that feeling of being somebody in this world, of belonging.

The thing she dreaded had finally come to pass: Sarah had become her cancer. She was her own tumor personified. No one saw the brilliant, elegant, high-performance, forty-something woman, only the embodiment of her illness. To them, she was no longer a lawyer who happened to be ill, she was a walking illness that happened to be a lawyer. It was an important difference.

Cancer scared people, it isolated them, pushed them away. It stank of death. People preferred to turn away, holding their noses.

Untouchable: that was what Sarah had become. Relegated to the margins of society.

And so no, she would not go back there, to the arena that had condemned her to death. They wouldn't see her fall. She wouldn't make a spectacle of herself, offer herself up to the lions. She still had one thing — her dignity. The power to say "no."

That morning, she hadn't touched the breakfast tray that Ron had prepared for her. The twins had come to kiss her before school, they had snuggled next to her in bed. She hadn't even responded to the touch of their small, warm, supple bodies. Hannah had begged her, trying everything to get Sarah up and out of bed: she had encouraged her, threatened her, made her feel guilty. But nothing worked. She knew she would find her mother in exactly the same place when she came home.

Sarah spent her days in a morbid, lethargic state; she felt increasingly numb. She drifted far away from the world. She thought back over the past few weeks in her mind, wondered what she might have done to change the course of things. Nothing, very probably. Play had gone on without her, and now it was game over. The end.

She had thought she could convince herself and everyone else that everything was fine, that nothing had changed. She had thought she could carry on as usual, stay on course, stand her ground, pretend. She had thought she could manage her illness, handle it like a new case, apply herself to the task methodically, and with determination. But it hadn't been enough.

In a waking dream, she pictured her colleagues' reactions to the news of her death. A macabre thought, but it pleased her, like choosing to listen to a sad song when you're feeling unhappy, just to feed your mood. She could imagine their tearful faces, their feigned sorrow. *The tumor was malignant,* they would say; or, *She knew this was the end. It was too late,* they would say, assigning the blame to her. *She waited too long to go to the doctor.* They would find her guilty of hastening her own end. But the truth was quite different. The thing that was killing Sarah Cohen, consuming her like a slow-burning fire, was not merely the tumor that had taken possession of her body and was leading her now in this dance of death, with its cruel, unpredictable twists and turns; no, the thing that was killing her was her desertion by the people she had considered her peers, in the firm whose reputation she had helped build. The firm had been her life's work, her reason to get out of bed in the morning, her *ikigai,* as the Japanese called it. Without it, Sarah no longer existed. She was a hollow creature, empty of substance, a weak, sick body.

Still, she was amazed at her own credulity.

She, who had feared her illness might unsettle things at work, was forced to confront a crueler reality: the firm was doing just fine without her. Her parking space would be reassigned, together with her office. People would fight for it hand over fist. And the thought destroyed her.

Concerned, her doctor had prescribed antidepressants. News-of-a-serious-illness-can-often-spark-depression-in-a-patient, he said. And depression-can-impact-negatively-on-the-evolution-of-a-patient's-cancer. Idiot, Sarah thought. She wasn't the only one who was sick. Society as a whole was in need of urgent treatment. The weak, the people that society ought to protect and support, were the very people it turned its back on, like the oldest elephants, left behind by the herd, condemned to a lonely death. She had read something once, in a children's book about animals: "Carnivores are useful in the natural world, because they eat the weakest and sickest animals." At this, her daughter had begun to cry. Sarah had consoled her, telling her that humans didn't live by the same rules. She had thought she was behind the barricade, in the civilized world. But she had been wrong.

They could prescribe as many pills as they liked, it wouldn't make the slightest difference, or hardly any. There would still be the Johnsons and Cursts of this world to push her back under.

Bastards, all of them.

The children had left for the day, the house was silent once again. Sarah got out of bed. Walking to the bathroom was all she could manage that morning. In the mirror, her skin was paper white and so thin it looked almost translucent. Her ribs jutted out; her legs looked like sticks, ready to snap if she tripped even slightly. Before, her legs had been shapely, her backside had been firm and round, encased in well-cut, slim-fitting suits; her neckline had been an acknowledged weapon of mass seduction. It was a fact: Sarah Cohen was highly attractive. Few men could resist her. She'd had a few flings, a few affairs, and she'd been in love twice — her two husbands, especially the first, the man she had loved so much. Who would find her attractive now, with her pale face and emaciated body, in the tracksuit that hung off her like a ghostly shroud?

The disease was sapping her strength. Soon, she would resort to wearing her daughter's things. Twelve years of age — that was all she'd be able to wear, children's sizes. Whose flame would she kindle then? At that moment, Sarah thought she would give anything to have someone take her in their arms. To feel like a woman, for a few more seconds. A woman in a man's arms. That would be sweet indeed.

Minus one breast — at first, she hadn't wanted to admit it, the pain, the sorrow. She had done what she always did and drawn a veil over it, in a vain attempt to distance herself, to push it back behind a screen. It was nothing, she had repeated to herself, plastic surgery can work wonders. But it was an ugly, dissembling word: mastectomy. Really, it was an amputation, a mutilation, an aberration. Perhaps, if she was lucky, it was a path to healing, too? Who could promise her that? When Hannah had heard the news of her mother's illness, she had looked very sad. She had thought for a moment, and then she had said: *Mom, you're an Amazon.* Sarah had smiled. Not long before, her daughter had written a school project on that very topic. She had corrected it herself. She remembered it now:

The word "Amazon" comes from the Greek *mazos* or mammary, preceded by "a," meaning "deprived of."

The Amazons were women in the ancient world who cut off their right breasts so that they would make better archers. They were a nation of warriors, both feared and respected. They reproduced with men from neighboring tribes but raised their children alone. They employed men as domestic servants. They fought in many wars and were often victorious.

Sarah was anything but certain she could win this war. The body she had pushed, ignored, neglected, even starved over the years — no time to eat, no time to sleep — was taking its revenge now, cruelly reminding her of its existence. Sarah was a shadow, a pale copy of her old self, reflected pitilessly, there in the mirror.

Her hair saddened her the most. It was coming out in handfuls now. The oncologist had warned her, like some grim oracle: it would start falling out after the second round of chemo. Sarah had found dozens of hairs strewn like fallen warriors over her pillow. She dreaded this more than anything. Hair loss was the embodiment of the disease. A bald woman was a sick woman, no matter if she sported a beautiful sweater, high heels, the latest must-have bag. No one would notice. That was all there was: the bald head, an admission, a confession, a symbol of suffering. A man with a shaved head could be sexy, but a bald woman would always be ill.

And so the cancer had robbed her of everything: her job, her looks, her femininity.

She pictured her mother, defeated by the same disease. She could go back to bed and slip away in silence, join her down there where she lay in the earth, share her eternal rest. It was a morbid yet comforting thought. It was soothing, in a way, to think that everything had an end, that the most unbearable torment could cease tomorrow.

When she thought of her mother, it was her elegance that she remembered. Even when she was ill and weak, her mother never appeared without makeup, her hair and nails always immaculate. Nails were an important detail, she had often said: always take care of your hands. Many would dismiss it as pointless preening, but to Sarah, like her mother, it was a symbol, a significant gesture: I still take time to look my best. I am a super-busy, working woman, I have responsibilities, three children (one cancer), I am consumed by my daily routine, but I haven't given up, I haven't disappeared, I'm here, still here, feminine and perfectly groomed, whole: see the tips of my fingers. I am here.

Sarah was here. In front of the mirror. She

gazed at her damaged nails, her thinning hair. At that very moment, she felt something resonate deep inside her, as if some tiny part of her refused the death sentence. No, she would not die. She would not give up.

She was an Amazon, a warrior, a fighter. An Amazon would never "let herself go." She would fight to her last breath. She would never give up.

She must return to the fight, take up the struggle once more. In her mother's name, in her daughter's name, and in the names of her sons, who needed her. In the name of all the wars she had waged. She must carry on. She would not lie down in that bed, not let herself sink into the arms of death. She would not be buried alive. Not today.

She dressed quickly. To cover her head, she grabbed a knitted hat from the cupboard — a child's hat that lay forgotten, with a superhero badge on the front. Never mind, it would keep her warm.

She left the house, dressed just as she was. It was snowing outside. She had thrown on a coat, over three sweaters piled one on top of the other. The clothes made her look tiny, like a Highland sheep staggering under the weight of its tangled fleece.

Sarah left the house. Today was the day, she had decided.

She knew exactly where to go.

GIULIA

Palermo, Sicily
Italian people want Italian hair.

The phrase dropped like a butcher's cleaver. In the living room of the family house, Giulia had just set out to her mother and sisters her plan to import Indian hair and save the workshop.

She had worked tirelessly to develop the project over the preceding days. She had studied the market, prepared a dossier for the bank — they would need money to invest in the scheme, obviously. She had worked day and night, barely slept, but she hadn't cared: she was on a mission, driven by a quasi-religious zeal. She had no idea where this newfound confidence, this sudden burst of energy, had come from. Was it Kamal's benevolent presence at her side? Was it her father, deep in his coma, passing his strength and conviction to her? Giulia was ready to move mountains, from the

215

Apennines to the Himalayas.

She wasn't spurred by the prospect of wealth, she cared nothing for the millions the English businessman boasted of. She didn't need a swimming pool or a helicopter. All she wanted was to save her father's workshop and keep a roof over her family's head.

It won't work, said Mamma. The Lanfredi have always bought their hair in Sicily. The *cascatura* is an ancestral custom here. Challenge tradition at your peril, she admonished.

Tradition will lead us to ruin, replied Giulia. The accounts are perfectly clear: the workshop will close in a month, at most. We need to rethink the production process, open it up to supplies from elsewhere. Accept this changing world and change with it. Family firms that refuse to move with the times are shutting down one after the other in Sicily. We need to expand our horizons, look further afield, it's a matter of survival! Adapt or die, there is no other choice. Speaking these words, Giulia felt wings sprouting at her back, as if she were suddenly a lawyer at the bar of a great courtroom, in an important trial. It was a profession that had always fascinated her — but a profession reserved for cultivated people,

216

from the upper echelons of society. There were no lawyers in the Lanfredi clan, only workers. But she would have loved to defend important causes in a court of law, to be a powerful, distinguished woman. She thought about it sometimes, and the thought joined all the others, in the limbo of her forgotten dreams.

Giulia spoke forcefully, enthusiastically. Indian hair had superb qualities, she said, a host of experts agreed. Asian hair is stronger, African hair is the most brittle, but Indian is best, for its texture, and its capacity to take color. Once the hair was discolored and dyed, it looked exactly like European hair in every way.

Francesca joined the discussion: she agreed with their mother, it would never work. Italians wouldn't want imported hair. Giulia was unsurprised. Her sister was one of the great skeptics of this world, the people for whom everything was black and gray, who always answered "no" before even considering "yes." Who always spotted the ugly detail in a landscape, the tiny stain on a fresh tablecloth; the people who pored over the surface of life in search of something to pick at, made it their reason for living, delighting in disaster. She was the opposite of Giulia, a true negative image:

Giulia's light was her darkness.

If Italians don't want Indian hair, we'll open up to other markets, said Giulia. The Americans, the Canadians. It's a big world out there, people need hair! Implants, extensions, and wigs were a fast-growing sector. They must catch the wave and ride it, not go under.

Francesca made her doubts — her resistance to the whole project, in fact — abundantly clear. She was the older sister, and she didn't mince her words. How was Giulia planning to go about it? She had never left Italy, never even been on a plane! Her world barely extended beyond the Bay of Palermo — how did she think she could pull off this extraordinary feat, this miracle?

But Giulia wanted to believe. The internet had made the world a much smaller place. Distance meant nothing; the world fitted in the palm of their hands today, like the globe lamp they had been given when they were children. India was so close — a whole subcontinent on their doorstep. She had studied the prices at length, she knew what to pay and what to charge, her scheme was workable. All it took was courage and faith. She had both.

Adela said nothing. She sat in a corner and watched her sisters argue — she remained neutral in any situation, indifferent to the world and everyone in it. A typical teenager.

We must close the workshop and sell the building, Francesca insisted. That would pay off part of the loan secured on the house. And what will we live on? demanded Giulia. Did she think it would be easy, finding another job? And their workers? Had she thought about them? What future for the women who had worked for them all for so many years?

The discussion was turning into a confrontation. Mamma knew she would have to intervene and separate her daughters, whose raised voices were echoing through the house. They had never understood one another, she thought bitterly. Their relationship had been a series of clashes, of which this was the biggest. She must speak, and make a decision, to settle the matter.

It is true, we must think of the workers, she said, that is a question of honor and respect. But Francesca is right on one point: Italian people want Italian hair.

Mamma's words sounded the death knell for Giulia's plan.

She left the house, utterly defeated. She had known she would have to justify the scheme, but she hadn't imagined meeting such fierce opposition. She felt like the morning after a party — sick and hungover from the heady intoxication of the night before. She could do nothing for the workshop without the agreement of her mother and sisters. They had demolished her castle in the air. Her tremendous enthusiasm had been eroded, and fear and doubt — the enemies of good judgment — had taken its place. She would take refuge at the hospital, at her father's bedside. What would he have said? What would he have done? She wanted so much to shelter in his arms, to cry for ages like a little child. Her faith was deserting her; she no longer knew what to do, whether to persevere with the plan or bury it, burn it on the altar of reason, in the name of traditions that were slowly dying. She felt beaten, exhausted, so tired from her sleepless nights that she could fall asleep there and then, on the hospital bed, next to Papà. She could sleep for a hundred years, like him. Yes, that was what she wanted.

Giulia closed her eyes.

Suddenly she was up there under the eaves, in the *laboratorio.* Her father was there, too, sitting and gazing out at the sea, like he always did. He didn't seem to be in pain. He looked serene, at peace. He smiled at Giulia as if he had been expecting her.

She sat beside him. She told him all her troubles, her sorrow, the feeling of powerlessness that gripped her. She told him she was sorry about the workshop.

Don't let anyone divert you from your path, he said. You must keep believing. You have great determination. I believe in your strength, your abilities. You must persevere. Life has great things in store for you.

A sharp noise rang out. Giulia woke with a start. She had fallen asleep right there, sitting beside her father in his hospital bed. Around him, the machines that kept him alive were sounding their alarms. Nurses were hurrying to his bedside.

At that moment, at that precise instant, Giulia swore she felt her father's hand move.

SMITA

Tirupati, Andhra Pradesh, India
Dawn is breaking over Tirumala mountain.

Smita and Lalita have rejoined the pilgrims lining up before the temple gates. A child steps forward and offers them *laddus,* round pastries made from dried fruit and condensed milk. Their weight and composition are strictly defined — the recipe was dictated by the god himself, says the boy. They are prepared inside the temple by the *achakas* — hereditary priests — who give them to the pilgrims. Eating them is part of the process of purification. Smita thanks Lord Vishnu for this providential feast. Revived by a few hours of sleep, and the sweet-tasting *laddus,* she feels ready for the sacrifices in store. She hasn't told Lalita what lies ahead, inside. The wealthiest pilgrims leave offerings of food and flowers, jewelery, gold, and precious stones, but the poorest offer Lord Venkateswara the only thing they possess: their hair.

It's a tradition dating back thousands of years: to offer your hair is to renounce all vanity, all sense of self, to lay yourself bare and come before the god in total humility.

Smita and Lalita enter the temple and begin their progress along the passages covered in wire mesh, where thousands of Dalits wait — as long as forty-eight hours, says a man sitting on the ground beside the entrance. The better-off buy tickets to jump the line. Whole families sleep in line, so as not to lose their place. After long hours in the makeshift cages, they come at last to the *kalyanakatta,* a huge building, four stories high, where hundreds of barbers are busy at work, night and day. The biggest barbershop in the world, people say. Smita learns that it costs fifteen rupees to shave your head. Truly, nothing in life is free.

In the vast room, as far as the eye can see, men, women with babies in their arms, children, and old people, all submitting to the razors, each chanting a prayer to Vishnu. The sight of the endless lines of shaved heads terrifies Lalita. She begins to cry. She doesn't want to give her hair away, she loves it. She hugs her doll for protection, the toy she has clung to throughout their journey, dressed in its scrap of cloth. Smita bends over her and whispers softly in her ear:

Don't be afraid.
Vishnu is with us.
Your hair will grow again — it will be even
   more beautiful than before.
Don't worry, I'll go first.

Her mother's soft voice offers Lalita some comfort. She stares at a group of children whose heads have just been shaved. They stroke their scalps with their hands and laugh. They don't seem to be suffering. The opposite, in fact — they seem amused by their new appearance. Their mother, her head freshly shaven, too, anoints them with sandalwood oil, a bright yellow liquid that is thought to protect the skin from the sun and from infections.

It is their turn. The barber signals to Smita. Devoutly, she steps forward as asked. She kneels, closes her eyes, and begins to recite a prayer in a low whisper. What she asks Vishnu, there in the midst of the vast hall, is her secret. It is a moment that belongs to her alone. She has thought about it for days; she has thought about it for years.

The barber manipulates his razor to quickly change the blade — the director of the temple is very strict, one blade per pilgrim, that's the rule. In his family, they have been barbers from father to son for generations. Every day, he performs the same gestures, repeats them over and over so that he even dreams about them at night. He imagines oceans of hair, in which sometimes he drowns.

He asks Smita to braid her hair — it makes the shaving easier, and the strands are easier to collect from the floor. Then he sprinkles her head with water and begins to shave. Lalita stares anxiously at her mother, but Smita smiles. Vishnu is with them, he is here, so close by. He is blessing her.

Smita closes her eyes again. There are thousands of people all around her, in the same pose, praying for a better life, offering the only thing that has been given to them in this world, their hair, the ornament, the gift they have received from heaven and which they now return, with joined hands, kneeling on the floor of the *kalyanakatta*.

When Smita opens her eyes, her scalp is as smooth as an egg. She stands up and feels suddenly, amazingly, light. It's a new, almost intoxicating sensation. A shiver runs through her body. She stares at the hair that was once hers, lying in a small, jet-black heap at her feet like a remnant of herself, already a memory. Now her body and soul are pure. She feels at peace. Blessed. Protected.

Lalita steps forward for her turn. She is trembling slightly. Smita takes her by the hand. The barber changes his blade and gazes admiringly at the braid reaching down the little girl's back, almost to her waist. Her hair is magnificent, thick, silky. Gazing into her daughter's eyes, Smita chants with her the prayer they have recited so many times before the little altar in their hut, in Badlapur. She thinks of their condition in life; she tells herself that they are poor now, but that perhaps, one day, Lalita will own a car. The thought makes her smile and gives her strength. Her daughter's life will be better than hers, thanks to the offering they are making here and now.

They emerge from the *kalyanakatta,* and the light dazzles their eyes. With no hair, their faces look more alike than ever. They seem younger, too, and more fragile. They hold hands and smile at one another. They have come this far. The miracle has been accomplished. Smita knows that Vishnu will keep his promise. A new life awaits them, tomorrow, with her cousins in Chennai.

Smita walks toward the Golden Sanctuary with Lalita's hand in hers. She feels no sadness. No, truly, she is not sad, because she is certain of one thing: they have made their gift, and Vishnu will show his thanks.

GIULIA

Palermo, Sicily
They did not know it was impossible, so they did it.

Giulia remembers Mark Twain's phrase, the one she had read and loved as a child. She thinks about it today, as she waits on the tarmac at Falcone Borsellino Airport. She feels moved, waiting for the plane that will change their lives. It is coming from so far away, bringing their first shipment of hair.

Papà never woke up. He died that day, in the hospital, while she sat in the chair beside him, after the strange dream that she would remember for the rest of her life. When it was time to go, he had pressed her hand, as if to say goodbye. As if to say, Go on. He had passed her the baton and left this life. Giulia knew that. While the doctors had tried to resuscitate him, she had promised him that she would save the workshop. It was their secret, his and hers.

She had insisted on holding the funeral in the chapel Papà loved. Her mother had protested — it was too small for everyone to have a seat, she said. Pietro had so many friends, he was always so popular, and there was all the family, too, from every corner of Sicily, and the workers . . . None of that mattered, Giulia told her. Anyone who loved him would stand. Her mother had given in, eventually.

She hardly recognized this new daughter: Giulia, who was ordinarily so well behaved, so self-contained, so docile, had become strangely obstinate. She was gripped by a new determination. She had stubbornly refused to give up her fight for the workshop. To break the deadlock, Giulia had suggested allowing the women to vote. It had been done elsewhere, she said, in other businesses under threat. They had every right to be consulted: it affected them, too. Her mother agreed, and her sisters had accepted the idea.

The vote took the form of a secret ballot, to avoid the younger women being influenced by their elders. The workers were invited to choose between a new direction for the workshop, with imported hair from India, or its closure and a negotiated severance package, with a small sum as compensation. The first solution involved an element of risk, of course: an uncertain outcome that Giulia made no effort to conceal.

The vote was held in the main workshop space. Mamma was present, together with Francesca and Adela. Giulia opened the ballot papers with trembling hands. Each had been folded and placed in Papà's old hat — that was her idea, a final tribute to her father. *So that he can be with us in a small way today,* she said.

There was a clear majority, seven votes to three. Giulia would remember that moment for years to come. She could barely conceal her joy.

Through Kamal she established a trusted contact in India, a man based in Chennai. He had studied business at the university and toured the country's temples looking for hair to buy. He struck a hard bargain, but Giulia proved a tough negotiator, too. *Mia cara,* anyone would think you had been doing this your whole life! chuckled La Nonna.

At just twenty years old, she found herself at the head of the workshop. She was the youngest business owner in the neighborhood. She has taken over her father's desk.

She gazes at his photograph on the wall, next to the pictures of their forebears. She hasn't dared add her own. That will come.

In her sadder moments, she goes up to the attic, to the *laboratorio* under the eaves. There, she sits facing the sea and thinks about her father, and what he would say, what he would do. She never feels alone. Her Papà is at her side.

Kamal stands beside her now. He insisted on coming with her to the airport. Lately, they have shared far more than their mid-day breaks. He has proved himself to be a source of tireless support, greeting each of her ideas with kind enthusiasm. He is inventive, enterprising. First, he was her lover, now he is her partner and confidant.

At last, the plane appears. Giulia watches the slowly growing dot in the sky and thinks that their whole future lies there, in the potbellied freight hold. She takes Kamal's hand. It seems to her now that they are no longer two separate beings, drifting through life by chance, but a man and a woman anchored to one another. It doesn't matter what Mamma says, or the family, or the neighborhood, Giulia thinks. She is a woman now, standing with the man who has revealed her true self. She will hold tight to this hand.

She will press it often in the years ahead, in the street, in the park, in the maternity wing, asleep, when they make love, when she cries, when she brings their children into the world. She will hold this hand for a long time to come.

The plane lands and comes to a halt. Speedily, the containers are unloaded and taken to the sorting hangar, where the warehousemen are busy at work.

In the storage depot, Giulia signs a receipt indicating that she has taken charge of the merchandise. The package is there in front of her, scarcely any bigger than a suitcase. With trembling hands, she takes a cutter and slits it open along one side. The first strands of hair appear. Delicately, she takes hold of a strand: long, very long, jet-black hair. A woman's hair, unquestionably, incredibly thick and sleek. And another strand, just beside it, not quite as long, and as soft as silk or velvet. A child's hair, by the feel of it. The batch was bought a month ago, at the temple in Tirupati, her contact told her: the busiest temple complex of any religion, anywhere in the world, busier than Mecca or the Vatican. Giulia had been impressed. Suddenly she thinks of all the men and women she doesn't know and will never meet, who come to give the gift of their hair. Their offering is a gift from God, she thinks. She wants to take them in her arms and thank them. They will never know where their hair has been taken to, its extraordinary journey, its odyssey. But the journey is just beginning. One day, someone, somewhere in the world, will wear the strands that her workers have disentangled, washed, and treated. That person will have no inkling of the struggles involved. She will wear this hair, and perhaps it will be her pride and joy, just as it is for Giulia, here today. With that thought, she smiles.

With Kamal's hand in hers, she has found her place in the world. Her father's workshop is saved. He can rest in peace. Their children will carry on the line, one day. She will teach them the trade and show them the roads she had ridden with Papà, on his Vespa.

Sometimes, the dream returns. Giulia is no longer nine years old. Her father's Vespa will never come back, but she knows now that the future is full of promise.

Now, the future is hers.

SARAH

Montreal, Canada
Sarah walks through the snowy streets. In
the Arctic freeze of early February, she
blesses the winter weather: it is her alibi.
Thanks to the cold, her woolly hat blends
with the crowd of passersby, each covered
up like her. She sees a group of schoolchildren holding one another by the hand. One
little girl wears a hat exactly like hers. They
catch one another's eye and grin.

Sarah keeps on walking. In the pocket of
her coat, she holds the small card given to
her by a woman she met at the hospital a
few weeks before. They had been sitting in
the same room waiting for their treatment
and had struck up a conversation, naturally,
like two strangers on a café terrace. They
had sat there chatting like that all afternoon,
united by their illness — the invisible thread
that bound them together. Their conversation had soon taken a more intimate, confes-

sional turn. Sarah had read a great many personal stories in forums and blogs online. Sometimes, she almost felt she was part of a club, an enlightened band of women who *knew,* and who had gone through *it.* There were the hardened warriors, the Jedi, who had seen it all before. And then there were the neophytes, new to the disease, the Padawans — the ones who, like Sarah, had everything to learn. That day, the woman at the hospital — a Jedi, no doubt about it, fighting yet another battle in a long war, though she drew a veil over her own illness — had talked about a shop that sold "spare hair," in her inimitable phrase. The staff were competent and discreet, she said. She had given Sarah a card with the salon's address, for *when the time came.* In the fight to get well, no woman should lose her self-esteem, she said. *The woman you see in the mirror should be your best friend, not your worst enemy,* she added, with a knowing wink.

Sarah had put the card away and thought no more about it. She had tried to put off the inevitable moment, just as she had tried to deny the illness itself for so long, but reality had caught up with her.

The time has come. Sarah walks to the salon through the snowy streets. She could have taken a cab, but she chooses to walk. It is a kind of pilgrimage, a journey she must make on foot, a rite of passage.

Going there means a lot. It means accepting the illness at last. Not rejecting it, not denying its existence. Looking it in the eye, facing it, not as a punishment or a twist of fate, an unavoidable curse, but as a fact, a life event, a challenge to overcome.

As she draws nearer to the salon, Sarah has a curious feeling, not exactly déjà vu, not a premonition, no, this is something deeper, something that filters softly into her thoughts, her entire being, as if she has already made this journey, as if she knows the way. And yet this is the first time she has ever ventured into this neighborhood. Inexplicably, it seems as if something is waiting for her there. Like a meeting that was arranged a long time ago.

She pushes the salon door. An elegantly dressed woman greets her politely and leads her along a hallway to a small room furnished with an armchair and a mirror.

Sarah takes off her coat and puts her bag down on the floor. She pauses before removing her woolly hat. The woman stands looking at her for a moment, saying nothing.

I'll show you our models. Do you have an idea of the kind of thing you're looking for?

Her voice is neither obsequious nor sympathetic. Straight and without affectation. Spot-on. Sarah immediately feels comfortable. Clearly, the woman knows what she's doing. She must meet dozens, hundreds of women like her. She probably sees them all day long. But right now, Sarah feels unique — or at least, that she is being treated as if she were. It's an art, not to dramatize or minimize, and this lady practices it with a delicate touch.

Sarah feels awkward as she struggles to answer the woman's question. She has no idea. She hasn't thought about it. She wants . . . something with life to it, natural. Something that looks like her, really. What a stupid thing to say, she thinks, how can someone else's hair "suit" her, match her face, her personality?

The woman disappears for a moment, then returns with what looks like a pile of hatboxes. From the first, she takes out an auburn wig — synthetic, she says, made in Japan. She shakes it out vigorously, top down. Sometimes they get a bit squashed in the box, she says, they need shaking to get them back into shape. Sarah tries it on, unconvinced. She doesn't recognize herself under the thick pile of hair. That isn't her under the fur ball, she looks like a person in disguise. Good value for money, the woman remarks. But it's not our premium range. She takes another wig from a second box, also artificial, but finer quality — from the "Top Comfort" range. Sarah doesn't know what to say. She stares thoughtfully at the image reflected back at her in the mirror. It is definitely not her.

The wig isn't bad, there's nothing wrong with it, but it *looks* like a wig. No, this is impossible, much better to wear a head scarf or a woolly hat. The woman takes a third box and produces one of her latest pieces, made with real hair, she notes. A rare and expensive model, but some women feel it's worth spending the money. Sarah stares at the wig in surprise. The hair is exactly the same color as her own. It is long, silky, and incredibly soft and thick. Indian hair, the woman tells her. It's treated, discolored, and dyed in Italy — at a family workshop in Sicily, actually. Then the strands are attached, one by one, onto a tulle cap, using the hand-tied braiding technique, she explains. It takes longer, but it's much stronger than a crochet wig. Eighty hours of work, around 150,000 individual hairs. This is a very fine, rare piece. Truly a *belle ouvrage,* as we say in the trade, she adds proudly.

She helps Sarah to position the wig —

always from front to back, it might seem a little tricky at first, but you'll soon get used to it, she says, you won't even need a mirror after a while. Of course, she can have it restyled to her taste, in a hair salon. Upkeep is simple, just shampoo and rinse, like your own hair.

Sarah lifts her chin and looks at herself in the mirror: a new woman stares back at her, a woman who looks just like her yet is someone different at the same time. It's a strange feeling. She recognizes her features, her pale skin, the dark shadows under her eyes. That's me, she thinks. Yes, it's really her. She touches the strands of hair, arranges them, models them, pushes them into shape: she isn't trying to make them her own, exactly, but to tame them. The hair shows no resistance. It is compliant, generous, it allows itself to be tamed. Slowly, it falls into place, framing her features. Sarah smooths it, strokes it, brushes it, surprised to find it so cooperative. She feels almost grateful to it. Imperceptibly, a stranger's hair is becoming her own; it matches her look, her silhouette, her features.

Sarah contemplates her reflection. Suddenly it seems this hair is restoring the things she has lost. Her strength, her dignity, her determination, the things that made her the woman she was. Sarah, proud and beautiful. She feels ready. She turns to the woman and asks if she can shave her head completely. She wants to do it, right there, right now. She can wear the wig from today on. She's not ashamed to go back home looking like this. And she'll be able to fit it on better without any hair underneath. It will be easier. It will have to be done sooner or later, at any rate, so she might as well get on with it now, here: she feels strong enough to do it today.

The woman agrees. Armed with a razor, her expert hands carry out the task gently and swiftly.

When Sarah opens her eyes, she stares in surprise for a moment. Newly shaven, her head looks smaller than before. She looks like her daughter at one year old, before her hair had grown. That's it — she looks like a baby. She tries to imagine her children's reaction — they will be surprised to see her like this. She will show them one day, perhaps. Later.

Or not.

She places the wig over her smooth scalp, using the technique the woman has shown her, then adjusts her new hair. Gazing at her reflection in the glass, Sarah knows one thing: she is going to live. She will see her children grow up. She will see them become adolescents, and adults, and parents. More than anything, she wants to know what their likes and dislikes will be, their talents and skills, their aptitudes, their loves. She will accompany them through life, be the attentive, tender, benevolent mother at their side.

She will win this fight, drained and exhausted, perhaps, but still standing. No matter how many months or years of treatment it takes, from now on she will devote all her energy, every minute, every second, to fighting this illness body and soul.

Never again will she be Sarah Cohen the powerful, confident woman that so many people admired. Never again will she be the invincible superwoman. She will be herself, Sarah, a woman who has been dealt a low blow by life, but she will be there, with her scars, and faults, and wounds. She won't try to hide them anymore. Her past life had been a lie, this life will be real.

When the illness grants her a reprieve, she will set up her own firm, with a few clients who still believe in her and are happy to follow her. She will take Johnson & Lockwood to court. She's a good lawyer, one of the best in town. She will make public the discrimination she suffered, in the name of the thousands of men and women written off by the world of work too soon, and who had endured, like her, a twofold penance. She will stand up for them. Doing what she does best. That will be her fight. She will learn to live differently, make time for her children, take days off to attend their school fetes and end-of-year shows. She won't miss a single one of their birthdays. She will take them on vacations, summers in Florida, winters skiing. No one will take those moments from her, they will be part of her life, too. There will be no more wall, no more lies. Never again will she be a woman cut in two.

Meanwhile, she must fight the mandarin with the weapons that nature has seen fit to grant her: her courage, her strength, her determination, her intelligence, too. Her family, her children, her friends. And the doctors, nurses, oncologists, radiologists, pharmacists, all of them fighting for her, every day, at her side. Suddenly it seems as if she is on the brink of an epic quest, carried along by an extraordinary energy. She feels a wave of warmth pass through her, a new effervescence, a sensation she has never felt before, like butterfly wings beating gently in her stomach.

Out there is the world, and her children. She will fetch them from school today. She

can picture their astonishment already —
it's something she's never done, or hardly
ever. Hannah will be very touched, no
doubt. The twins will run to her. They will
comment on her new hair. And Sarah will
explain it all. Everything. The mandarin,
her work, the war they will fight together.

As she leaves the salon, Sarah thinks of
the woman who gave up her hair, of the
Sicilian workers who disentangled and
treated it, with such infinite patience. She
thinks of the woman who assembled the
wig. She feels as if the whole world is working to help her heal. She remembers the
phrase from the Talmud: *Whoever saves one
life saves the world entire.* Today, the whole
world is saving her, and Sarah is filled with
gratitude.

She is here today, yes, right here, and she
will be here for a long time to come.

As she walks away with that thought, she
smiles.

EPILOGUE

My work is finished.
The wig is there, in front of me.
The feeling that overwhelms me is
    something unique.
No one has seen it yet.
This joy is mine alone.
The pleasure of a task completed.
Pride in a job well done.
Like a child who has finished a drawing, I
    smile.

I think of this hair,
Of the place it has come from, the
    journey it has made
And the journey it will make now.
A long road, I know.
One I will never see, shut up here in my
    workshop.
But that doesn't matter.
The journey is mine, too.
I dedicate my work to these women,

Bound by strands of hair,
Like a great net of souls.
To women who love, and give birth, and
    hope,
And fall and get back on their feet, a
    thousand times,
Who bend but never break.
I know their struggles.
I share their tears and their joy.
Each of them is a part of me.

I am one small link,
A hyphen connecting their lives,
A tenuous thread,
Thin as a strand of hair.
Invisible to the world, to the human eye.

Tomorrow I shall set to work once again.
Other stories are waiting.
Other lives.
Other pages.

ACKNOWLEDGMENTS

To Juliette Joste, for her enthusiasm and confidence.

To my husband, Oudy, for his indefatigable support.

To my mother, my very first reader, from childhood.

To Sarah Kaminsky, who encouraged me at every stage of the writing of this book.

To Hugo Boris, for his invaluable help.

To Françoise at L'Atelier Capilaria in Paris, for opening the doors of her workshop to me, and explaining her trade.

To Nicole Gex and Bertrand Chalais, for their wise counsel.

To the librarians at the Inathèque, who assisted me in my research.

And lastly, to my French teachers, throughout my school life and ever since, for giving me my love of writing.

ABOUT THE TRANSLATOR

Louise Rogers Lalaurie translates literary and genre fiction from French. Her work has been short-listed for the Crime Writers' Association International Dagger, the Best Translated Book Award, and the Jan Michalski Prize for Literature.

ABOUT THE AUTHOR

Laetitia Colombani comes from the world of film, where she has worked as a screenwriter-director and as an actress. She also writes for the stage. The international bestseller *The Braid* is her first novel.

The employees of Thorndike Press hope you have enjoyed this Large Print book. All our Thorndike, Wheeler, and Kennebec Large Print titles are designed for easy reading, and all our books are made to last. Other Thorndike Press Large Print books are available at your library, through selected bookstores, or directly from us.

For information about titles, please call:
(800) 223-1244

or visit our website at:
gale.com/thorndike

To share your comments, please write:
Publisher
Thorndike Press
10 Water St., Suite 310
Waterville, ME 04901